THUNDER STRUCK

THUNDER STRUCK

MARIE LONG

USA TODAY BESTSELLING AUTHOR

VanÆsir

Thunderstruck
(VanAesir, book 1)

Cover design by Fiona Jayde Media

Printed in the United States of America

10 9 8 7 6 5 4 3 2 1

ISBN: 978-1-9602530-4-0 (paperback)
ISBN: 978-1-9602530-3-3 (eBook)

THUNDER STRUCK

Chapter One

Tor Hagen peered through the gaps of the outdoor stage's crisscrossing steel scaffolding at the shouting, rowdy, headbanging crowd clamoring for an encore from the band onstage, Stingray Armageddon. The five-member group was a household name in Los Angeles's underground death metal community and was among Tor's most admired bands. It boggled his mind that such an elite band wasn't headlining. But at the annual Death by Metal festival, the bands performed in no particular order.

From his vantage point backstage, the crowd, which appeared to be two thousand strong, seemed daunting. A layer of sweat formed on Tor's palms. He swallowed, his heart beginning to pound. No one outside of Seattle really knew about VanAesir. How in Helheim was his trio expected to top Stingray Armageddon?

Tor inhaled a long, deep breath. The members of Stingray Armageddon took a bow, and the open field echoed with approving screams and roars.

Someone slapped Tor on the shoulder, and he looked back at his drummer, protégé, and best friend, Luca Ingram.

"Dude, you're just making things worse for yourself, looking out there," Luca said, giving him an amused grin.

Tor clenched his jaw. "How are you not nervous, having to perform right after them?"

Luca chuckled. "I'm excited, not nervous. This could be our big ticket to go places, y'know?"

"By putting us right after Stingray Armageddon? Who assembled this crazy line-up?"

"Who cares? We're finally getting the exposure we deserve. Let's give that crowd a reason to love us." Luca spun one of his wooden drumsticks between his fingers.

"Just don't blow up the amps again." Frida Winters adjusted the strap on her gold-and-chrome six-stringed bass then fluffed out the feathers of her black bolero. The amber gemstones of her golden necklace twinkled under the overhead stage lights. She fixed Tor with a stern look. "If you don't want to foot the bill for another damaged piece of stage equipment, control your damned powers this time."

Exasperated, Tor raked his fingers through his hair. He and his friends were part of a small population of the world who possessed certain powers or abilities that manifested during puberty. The phenomena most commonly happened to those who had an affinity for the arts. For Tor, it was electric energy that sometimes got channeled into whatever he was touching if he got too deep into the music. On stage, that meant his beloved electric guitar, Myollnir.

"What're you talking about, Fri?" Luca said. "The crowds love it when Tor goes berserk on stage. It's, like, our band's gimmick now."

"I don't want to be known as a fucking circus act," Frida retorted. "Besides, Harold will be furious if we screw up our PR."

Luca raised his eyebrows. "You'd rather Tor go back to playing drums, then?"

Tor cringed, remembering the first time his powers had manifested during VanAesir's early years, when he'd started his career as drummer. He'd played fast and furious, and the thunderous sounds, amplified by his powers, reached an overwhelming volume, shattering every sound system. No drum shield or booth could contain the acoustic thunder Tor produced when he'd let loose, which hindered the band's ability to create a decent song. As a result, Tor had retired from the drums and taken up lead guitar, which had quickly become his new love.

"Oh, gods, no." Frida sneered.

Laughing, Luca took out another drumstick from his belt. "Yeah, I'm a way better drummer, anyway."

Tor gave him a look. "I taught your sorry ass how to play drums!"

"Don't hate because the student surpassed the master."

The stage lights dimmed, and as Stingray Armageddon began unplugging and packing up their equipment, the event's emcee, a young man with dozens of steel rings in his eyebrows, nose, and lips, ran out.

"What a kickass performance!" he boomed into the microphone. He threw up his hands and shook his head. The ends of his long, scraggly black hair cinched with a black bandana whipped across his face. The volume of the roaring crowd increased.

Backstage, Tor watched the last member of Stingray Armageddon leave, and the event's tech crew and volunteer workers rushed on stage and began setting up the microphones, amplifiers, and Luca's ten-piece drum kit. After the crew left, Tor took a deep breath and nodded to his bandmates.

Luca bounced on his heels. "Let's go!"

"You guys are in for another treat tonight!!" the emcee shouted as he paced the dimly lit stage under a following spotlight.

Tor, Luca, and Frida hustled out and got in place. Tor stepped up to his standing microphone, took one look at the crowd, and swallowed.

He wiped his clammy hands on his black jeans. He glanced sideways at Frida, who stood at the other mic, her head held high and fingers poised on her bass, ready to play. She didn't acknowledge him and appeared deep in her own world. *At least* she's *not nervous.*

"This year's Death by Metal event is proud to present one of the hottest up-and-coming Viking death metal bands on the West Coast!" the emcee announced.

Tor looked over his shoulder at Luca, who sat behind his drum set. Luca caught his gaze, smirked, and nodded, as if he already had a plan in place if things went south during the set.

"It's time! For! Vaaannn-Ae-seer!" The emcee hurried backstage. The stage lights went full up, bathing Tor and his friends in cool blue and white light. Luca tapped his drumsticks, setting the tempo, and together, the three of them launched into one of their most popular songs—"War Edda."

Tor played the opening verse, strumming hard and growling the guttural war-chant lyrics into the microphone. He listened to the song in his mind, having played it repeatedly during practice and gigs, and his hands strummed autonomously while he let the music possess him.

Out of the corner of his eye, he noticed his hands emanating a soft white glow. He shook out of his brief trance and forced himself to be conscious of his playing again. The glow from his hands dissipated. But it wasn't long before he slipped back into his trance, and as he strummed the lead-in to the second verse, a spark fizzled from his fingers. In between verses, he cringed, trying desperately to reel in his powers. Goose bumps made his skin prickle, and he shivered from a sudden rush of static shock. As the feeling subsided, Tor glanced at Frida, who returned an icy glare.

I can't lose control now. I won't *lose control.* His teeth sinking into his bottom lip, Tor broke into a riff. The crowd went wild, headbanging and jumping around to the beat, throwing up hand signs, and screaming as the power and energy of the song began firing them up. Tor began chanting the lyrics of the next verse and entered his musical trance as the music took hold of him once more. He no longer saw the thousands of raving metalheads before him, but the empty, dark field beneath an overcast sky reminiscent of his recurring dreams.

"Alone he stands, ready for war. The gods are watching. From the depths of Muspelheim, the demons emerge…"

Tor blinked. For a moment, he was back on stage, playing. He bobbed his head, an auburn curtain concealing his face as he reached the bridge of the song, belting the lyrics in a low rumble. The music enveloped him, and he was back in his dream world, alone in the barren snowy field, looking up at the swirling clouds that threatened to unleash a hellish storm.

The white ground began to tremble, and a figure slowly emerged, its growing shadow rising higher,

higher. Tor's heart pounded in tune to the music's tempo. Sweat poured down his forearms as he tilted his head back farther, farther. The shadowy mass resolved into a giant blue-grey-skinned creature that loomed over him, dwarfing him. Parts of its muscular body were intricately formed into spiked leather-like mythical armor. Tor couldn't see the creature's face, but he felt a sense of familiarity. The giant appeared whenever Tor entered this world. Whenever Tor played Myollnir. As if the music were a beacon for this unstoppable force. Like a curse Tor could never break.

And yet, Tor could not stop playing. The music kept driving him. Calling to him. Enveloping his conflicting mind in a haze that kept him in the seemingly unbreakable trance.

"Drive them from the depths, by his thunderous reign. To Jotunheim, to the giants' domain…"

Part of Tor's subconscious sensed he was nearing the end of the song. His heart thrummed, anticipating what came next, and he wanted so desperately to suppress that feeling. He couldn't lose control. Not tonight.

The giant extended its massive hand, and an equally large battle-axe appeared. The giant grasped the axe's handle and stood poised, ready to attack.

The clouds formed ominous snakelike puffs, lighting up the sky with soft lightning, as if taunting him. Tor's forearm tickled as the hairs stood on end in anticipation. The storm watched and waited.

"*From the wasteland. We strike. We strike. To the death. We strike.*"

A bolt of lightning shot down from the ominous sky, hitting the ground just inches from the giant's bare feet. Tor's vision blurred in and out of reality. The barren land was electrified in a strange energy that drew him to the song's final release.

"*Warriors, take up arms! We strike. We strike. We strike! We striiike!*"

Tor growled at the top of his lungs, losing himself in his guitar solo. The image of the present world suddenly shifted, becoming one with the mythical world. His hands tingled, and he attacked Myollnir's strings as he marched around the stage with furious, deliberate steps.

More lightning rained down from the sky, striking everywhere except the giant. A bolt struck somewhere into the crowd of the present world, but it seemed to pass through the stands like a ghost. Tor concentrated, fists clenched, his vision becoming a blue electric haze. The present world fizzled away, and he was once again standing in the voids of the mythical world. Fully charged and in a blissful state of uncontrolled freedom, Tor ran toward the giant as it swung its axe.

Then the mythical world fizzled to blackness.

At the outro, Tor roared and fell to his knees on stage, picking the final chord, the sounds blaring from the speakers. A rush of electric energy surged throughout his body, bleeding from his fingers, into Myollnir. The current was channeled through the guitar's wire and straight into the amplifier.

Boom!

He jolted out of his trance, breathing heavily, sweat pouring down the sides of his face. He was back in the present world, before the immense, rowdy crowd, who gave a deafening cheer. Sparks flew from the back of the amplifier sitting near him. An ear-piercing screech reverberated from one of the overhead speakers, then it exploded, showering sparks onto the stage. Tor jumped back as sparks landed near his feet while the crowd's cheering continued. Tor looked to Frida, who glared at him. Luca grinned widely and gave him a thumbs-up.

The stage went dark. A spotlight appeared and focused on the emcee, who scrambled back on stage. "Holy shit, folks! VanAesir literally brought the house down!"

"VanAesir! VanAesir!" The chant pounded the air like thunder reinforced with stomping and clapping, demanding an encore.

"Sorry, guys, but that's all from them for tonight." He glared over his shoulder at Tor then turned back to the now-booing crowd. "We need to fix some technical difficulties before the next band. Sit tight, guys. I promise you, this night's about to get wild!"

The boos from the crowd grew louder as three tech crew members rushed past and began tending to the blown amplifier. Another crew member began scaling one of the scaffolds.

The emcee turned off the microphone and approached Tor. "Get the hell out of here before you destroy something else." He thumbed toward the exit.

Tor stared at the emcee. He couldn't even keep it together for one song. Clenching his jaw, he yanked the cable from his guitar, stormed past Frida and Luca, and grabbed his guitar case. Backstage, he discovered the remaining three bands who were waiting to play, all wearing confused looks on their faces.

"Oh man, what happened out there?" one of the band members asked him.

Ignoring the question, Tor brushed past them and headed straight for the barricaded lot filled with the performers' cars, tour buses, RVs, and trailers, which were parked in haphazard rows.

"One of the tech crew said an amp was blown," Tor heard another person say.

"Damn, so the rumors were true about VanAesir? No wonder people hate playing after them."

Gritting his teeth, Tor yanked open the door to the small trailer that was hitched to VanAesir's rental SUV. He laid Myollnir in its case and set the case inside the trailer. Shutting the door, he swore repeatedly. *I did it again. I fucking did it again!* He got into the driver's seat of the vehicle and ran his hands over his face, exasperated. The remnants of ozone scent on his hands reminded him of the disaster on stage.

His fingers slid down his face, and his eyes were suddenly drawn to a bottle of Warrior's Stout, his favorite beer, sitting in the console's cup holder. *How'd that get there?* He could definitely use a beer right about now. He swiped up the brown bottle and brought it to his lips.

"Dude! Stop kissing your phone and get out here!"

Tor jumped in his seat and frowned at Luca, who stood outside the driver's side window, smirking. Tor looked back at his beer and realized he was holding his cell phone. He threw the phone back into the console's cup holder, and opened the door. "Damn it, Luca, stop with your fucking illusions."

Luca shrugged innocently. "I don't know what you're talking about."

"Don't start…"

Luca held his hands up in surrender. "We're not done here, yet. We still got our fans to impress."

Tor shook his head. "We're done. We've been kicked out."

"What are you talking about? The crowd *loved* us! They're still chanting our name. Let's get back out there and give them an encore!"

"With what sound system?" Frida said, climbing into the passenger seat and slamming the door.

Tor's shoulders slumped, and he gave Frida an apologetic look. "Hey, I'm sorry, Fri. I—"

"One song!" she broke in. "We couldn't even get through one fucking song before you completely destroyed our chance of success!" She crossed her arms and sulked. The feathers of her bolero rose, as if echoing her anger.

Tor sighed. She was right. He'd screwed things up. *Again.* How much longer until she ended up quitting the band because of it? His heart ached at the thought. She was the lifeblood of the band. There was no VanAesir without the complementing vibes of Frida's bass. She was irreplaceable. And Tor would go insane if he had to retire Myollnir for good. "I'll fix this somehow, Fri," he said. "I swear, I will."

Frida looked at him, a mix of sadness and hurt in her dark-brown eyes. "I'm tired of waiting for you to 'fix it.' Maybe I'd be better off on my own."

Tor swallowed. If she hadn't already made up her mind, she was definitely considering it. He said nothing more and turned back to Luca. "Is everything packed? I'm heading back to the hotel."

Luca's bright expression went dark. "Seriously? We're leaving at a time like this?" He paused and rolled his eyes, letting out an exasperated sigh. "Fine. Let me get the rest of the drums packed."

Moments after Luca disappeared, Tor's cell phone buzzed on the console. He flinched, then reluctantly picked it up and checked the lit-up screen. Seeing his band manager's name, Harold Larssen, he made a sour face. *Shit. He already knows.* "What's up, Harold?" Tor answered in a casual voice.

"Just got back from having drinks with the owner of Smashed Keys Entertainment. He's pretty hyped about you guys and has invited you to play at Valhalla Injection this Saturday."

Tor's jaw dropped. *Valhalla Injection.* It was his dream to perform at the three-day-long annual Viking metal showcase world tour, but it was strictly by invitation only. "Holy shit. Are you serious?"

"I wouldn't be calling you if I wasn't," Harold said. "We've a lot of work to do till then. The money you guys earn tonight can go toward some new threads and gear."

Tor swallowed. *So he doesn't know?* "Uh…"

"Joel gave you your payment, right?"

"Oh, yep. He did. I took care of it."

There was a brief silence. "Right. Well, in the meantime, why don't you three mingle with your fans for a while, then meet me back at the hotel when you're ready?" Tor noticed a slight edge in the man's tone this time.

The line went dead before Tor could respond. Very little got past the older man, who possessed an extraordinary sense of perception that far exceeded any normal human's. Harold was so adept at his gift,

Tor swore the man could probably read minds if he wanted to.

Tor stared at his phone's screen until it dimmed.

"How pissed is Harold now?" Frida asked, staring out the passenger-side window.

Tor returned the phone to the console. "He doesn't know."

"Bullshit. Of course he knows. He *always* knows."

"Not this time. Actually, he had awesome news. He got us booked for Valhalla Injection this Saturday."

Frida's head snapped to him. She stared wide-eyed. "What did you say?"

Tor nodded. "I couldn't believe it myself. It's for real. We're actually playing at this year's Valhalla Injection!"

Her face lit up for a moment then went dark again. She turned her head and focused out her window. "There's no point in going. It'll just be another disaster. You're bad luck, Tor. You'll destroy the equipment again and fuck up everyone's weekend."

Tor frowned. "I told you I'll fix this. I'll find a way to ground my powers."

She shook her head. "There's nothing strong enough to ground you. Look. I'm done. I just want to go back to the hotel and forget about tonight."

"But Harold wanted us to go out and mingle with our fans before we went back to the hotel."

"I'm not in the mood to mingle. Take me back to the hotel. Now."

Tor exhaled through his nose. The sounds of the metal doors to their trailer opening drew his attention to the rearview mirror. Luca stood by and watched some of the volunteer workers load up all the pieces to his drum kit then secure the door. Luca returned to the SUV and hopped in the backseat. His normally cheery expression remained gloomy.

Tor drove off in silence. He made his way down a narrow paved road that led out of the festival field and onto the main road. It wasn't until the view of the festival field had disappeared from the rearview mirror that Tor finally informed Luca of Harold's news.

"Dude! We need to get our shit together and practice! This is gonna be awesome!" Luca blurted, his face lighting up again.

Tor glanced at Frida, who remained in her same position, staring out the window in silence. He wanted to say something to her, anything. But he feared whatever words came out of his mouth would only hasten VanAesir's inevitable demise.

 Chapter Two

Tristan Westgard watched through his mini-binoculars as the taillights of VanAesir's SUV became a tiny red blur in the distance. Then he banged his head against the passenger seat's headrest of the camper van and sighed. He couldn't get Frida's thick, wild hair, smooth tawny skin, and perfectly curvy body out of his head. Everything about her defined true beauty. He thought about their encounter earlier tonight. After VanAesir's short-lived performance, Tristan had caught up with her just as she was storming off after Tor and Luca.

"Frida," Tristan had called, his fingers grazing her arm as she'd brushed past him backstage.

She paused and spun, whipping her hand back. The amber gemstones of her necklace twinkled in the light. She glared icily at him. "What do you want, Tristan?"

"Just wanted to say that you were awesome out there."

She rolled her eyes. "Yeah, until Tor fucked things up, as usual."

Tor. Tristan sneered. "You're better than that. You'll never get ahead staying in VanAesir. Start your own band, or why not join another?"

She lifted an eyebrow. "Are you insinuating I should join Jotnar Malice?"

While the thought had been tempting, that was the last thing he wanted. Frida being in his band meant that he could never be her boyfriend. "No, I'm not saying that at all."

"Good, because I wouldn't be caught dead playing in your shitty band." She rolled her eyes.

Feisty. Tristan grinned, her resistance sending waves of delightful shivers down his spine. Tristan adored the way Frida played cat-and-mouse, unlike the random women and avid female fans who shamelessly threw themselves at him, hoping to get lucky. Frida carried herself with class, grace, and style. She knew her worth, and Tristan knew he would have to work for her prize. The mere thought was an instant turn-on for his competitive heart. "Hey, anywhere is better than the shit you're in now," he said, deliberately falling for her bait. "You're a damn good bassist."

She gave him a pathetic look. "It's my life, my career. I'll decide what I do."

"I know you will. That's why I wanna see you go far. You, of all people, deserve it."

"Huh." She glanced out into the parking lot in the distance then back at Tristan. "Well, at least someone around here thinks I do." She pulled out her cell phone and checked the screen. "Gotta go."

Bye, Frida. He watched her run off, phone in hand. She bumped into Dahlia Simons, his keyboardist, and dropped her phone in the grass. It bounced and landed at Dahlia's feet. The two women exchanged glares, then Dahlia picked up the phone and handed it to Frida. She swiped it from Dahlia's hands and stuffed it into her back pocket. After an exchange of words and another round of stares, the women turned and went their separate ways. Frida had disappeared in the sea of vehicles parked in the roped-off parking area of the open field. Frowning, Dahlia had walked toward Tristan, giving him a thumbs-up.

Blinking back to the present, Tristan slipped his hand in his pocket and pulled out a small black-velvet box. He flipped open the top and admired the pair of golden earrings etched with Nordic knot work. He'd carefully selected the earrings to match her alluring, beloved golden necklace, which she was never seen without. *One day, Frida…*

"Not again!"

Tristan shut the box and slipped it back into his pocket. He frowned at his older sister, the band's vocalist. Scarlet was leaning against the door, her forearms resting atop the rolled-down window. She regarded him with an icy hazel gaze.

"Not in the mood for your shit, Scarlet," Tristan warned.

"You look like a puppy-eyed idiot. Frida doesn't want anything to do with your sorry ass. Give it a rest."

Tristan gritted his teeth. "No, she'll be my girlfriend someday."

"Too late. She's stuck on Tor." Smirking, Scarlet drew a fiery heart shape in thin air with her finger. It fizzled into a wispy heart-shaped smoke ring and dissipated.

Remembering the brief conversation from earlier, Tristan shook his head. "He'll never get her."

"If Tor doesn't get her, then someone else will, and that someone most definitely won't be you."

He gritted his teeth, his blood boiling at the thought of some random guy putting his hands all over Frida, kissing her, and having his way. "I'm done, Scarlet."

"Hey, I'm just looking out for my little brother."

"Keep convincing yourself of that bullshit."

She fumed, her pupils briefly going alight with flames before returning to normal. "Frida is a shitty bassist in a shitty band with no chance of ever getting a record deal. You keep pursuing her, and she'll drag you right down with her."

He slammed his fist on the console, creating a small crack in the hard plastic. "Enough!" He took a deep breath, reeling in his power. "Go get the others. I'm ready to get out of here."

"Whatever." She pushed herself off the door and disappeared among the rest of the vehicles.

Tristan took another breath to calm his nerves, then he stared through his binoculars again, with some glimmer of hope that he would still see those taillights. They were long gone, though.

No matter. The hidden tracker Dahlia had placed on Frida's phone would allow Tristan to locate her. *But once I find her, how can I get her to look my way?* He had to get rid of Tor somehow. Or maybe find a way to convince Frida to leave VanAesir.

The driver's-side door flung open, and Tristan's drummer, Zeke Matsen, climbed in. The rest of the band, Eric Jacobsen, Dahlia, and Scarlet, piled into the backseats.

"Finally," Zeke said, starting up the van and tearing out of the parking area. "I'm starving. Is there any place open after midnight?"

"Stop thinking about food and pay attention to the road," Tristan growled. "And slow the fuck down! If my guitar ends up getting scratched in that trailer, I'm gonna break your neck."

Zeke grumbled and eased his foot off the gas.

"Dahlia, did you get the location?" Tristan peered toward the farthest backseat, where light scraping sounds penetrated the air.

Dahlia, who was casually filing her nails, paused and met his gaze. She pulled out her phone and checked the screen. A tiny electric spark emanated from her hand. "World Tree Hotel," she said then put her phone away.

Tristan nodded to Zeke. "Head there."

Zeke furrowed his brow. "What for?"

"I have some unfinished business."

"But I'm tired. And hungry."

"Shut up and drive."

Eric took out his earplugs and leaned in between Tristan and Zeke from the backseat. "Sooo… you ask her out yet?"

Tristan glared at his bassist.

"What?"

"This is Frida we're talking about. You don't 'ask' her anything. She makes her own decisions." Forcing her to go out with him would ruin everything he found so alluring about her, but that didn't mean he couldn't try to persuade her to make the decision he desired her to.

Dahlia snorted. "We need to be focused on more important things, like Valhalla Injection."

"Yeah, so let's head back to our *own* place instead of some random ritzy one," Zeke grumbled.

"No, it's all part of the plan," Tristan said.

"What plan?"

"The plan to ensure Tor's band doesn't make an appearance at Valhalla Injection." VanAesir and Jotnar Malice's deep rivalry had them constantly at odds with topping the charts of Seattle's underground metal music scene.

"Enlighten us, little brother," Scarlet said.

"Think about it. With VanAesir out of the way, we'd be sure to win the Battle of the Bands."

"Battle of the Bands," Zeke repeated, grinning. "I'd sure love to get my hands on that fifteen-grand cash prize."

"Wouldn't we all," Scarlet added. "But the guaranteed record deal is the most important part of that prize. Winning that contest will set us up for life. Think big, guys!"

"I always think big." Zeke chuckled deviously.

Scarlet rolled her eyes. "Yeah, as big as your peanut mind."

"So what are we gonna do about VanAesir?" Eric asked. "The crowd'll blow their loads as soon as Tor goes berserk on stage. VanAesir will win out of pure fandom."

Rubbing his chin, Tristan stared out the passenger's window at the passing streetlights. He changed his mind about talking to Frida directly, and a new idea for persuading her to leave VanAesir for good started to form. *What if Tor disappointed his fans and couldn't perform?* He smirked.

"I know that look," Scarlet said, interrupting his thoughts. "What are you scheming, little brother?"

Tristan turned to his friends. "We're going to eliminate the real competition. Make Myollnir disappear, at least from Tor."

Scarlet, Eric, and Dahlia looked at him dubiously.

"What are you talking about?" Eric said.

"Ever notice how disaster only happens whenever Tor is playing that guitar? That's got to be the source of his power."

"Have you forgotten the days when he was VanAesir's drummer?" Scarlet interjected. "The destruction was far worse."

"Yeah, but the band couldn't produce a decent song if their life depended on it. Back then, *we* were number one on the local charts." He thought about the years he'd spent studying his nemesis, Tor. "Those drums couldn't manipulate Tor's powers the way Myollnir can. It's like that guitar is a direct source of his power. When Tor goes berserk, it's as if he's channeling his emotions through the electrical energy he creates."

Eric furrowed his brow. "And you're saying the crowd feeds off that energy?"

"A crowd full of crazy metalheads? Absolutely."

"So how exactly are we going to make Myollnir disappear?" Zeke asked, not taking his eyes off the road.

"We take it." Tristan nodded.

"Wait. You want to steal Tor's *guitar*?"

"And even if we did steal it, what's stopping Tor from finding another guitar to play?" Scarlet added.

"I hope he does," Tristan said. "It'll fuck up his head big time. He'll be so busy thinking about the loss of his precious Myollnir that he won't be able to concentrate."

Scarlet's face brightened. "I get it now. Kill Tor's morale. Kill the band's performance."

"Kill their chances of winning." Tristan smirked.

"So that's the real reason why we're going to the World Tree Hotel?" Zeke made a face. "Wait. How did you even know they'd be there, anyway?"

"The hidden tracker I stuck on Frida's phone emits an electromagnetic pulse I can trace," Dahlia said, her eyes emanating a brief, flickering purplish glow.

"I can't believe we're actually going to steal Myollnir," Scarlet muttered, and then grimaced at Tristan. "You know Tor is gonna kick your ass for this, when he finds out, right?"

Tristan cracked his knuckles. "And I'll be eagerly waiting for him to try." Grinning, he shifted more comfortably in the passenger's seat. He wasn't just going to take Myollnir; he was going to master it. Something about that guitar's sound enticed fans. If Tristan tapped into its secrets, he would be unmatched as the greatest guitarist in the underground metal world. "Let's go get Myollnir."

Chapter Three

Tor and his friends parked in the back lot at the exquisite World Tree Hotel. They got out of the SUV, and Luca went around back to the trailer.

"What are you doing?" Tor asked.

Luca paused, his key inserted into the trailer door's lock, and looked over his shoulder. "I've thought about what happened tonight. We had the loudest cheer from the entire crowd—even louder than Stingray Armageddon. Can you believe it?"

Tor shook his head. "It's all in your head. We disappointed our fans, because of me."

"No! They loved us. They wanted more! But that dickhead emcee had to go and get us kicked off."

"How could we give them more with a blown amp?" Frida interjected. "Look, just drop it. I don't want to talk about tonight anymore."

Luca opened the trailer door. "Tor, whatever it is that's making you go berserk, keep doing it. The crowd loves you for it. You weren't able to do that on the drums."

Tor scratched his head. "You're not making sense." *Then again, since when did Luca ever make sense?*

"It's happened too many times. I wanna know the secret. *Your* secret. It's not just your power. It's Myollnir, too, isn't it?"

Tor blinked. "Well…"

"I want to see—"

"We're not unloading until we get home," Frida said, smacking Luca's hand off the trailer door handle and slamming the door shut. "It's bad enough that damaged amp will probably be coming out of our paychecks. I don't need another reason for Harold to go apeshit if Tor breaks something in this expensive-ass hotel."

Tor still couldn't believe Harold had booked them in such a high-end hotel. In Tor's experience, ritzy five-star places seemed to turn their noses up at so-called good-for-nothing young riff-raff metalheads like them. Luckily for them, the hotel's owner happened to be one of their biggest fans. Tor had never experienced so much royal treatment in his life. *Is this how all the famous musicians live every day?*

Frida snatched the key out of the lock and dropped it down the front of her black button-down blouse.

Tor and Luca stared at her, wide-eyed. Of course she had to hide it *there*—the one place where stealing it back would be damn near impossible. He valued his fingers—his *life*—too much to even attempt it.

Luca sighed and rubbed the back of his head. "Well, there goes *that* idea…"

Frida gave him a look. "Come on, you two."

Frowning, Luca leaned against the back of the trailer and crossed his arms. "I can't believe you're not the least bit curious about this, Fri. We've never really delved into the secrets of Tor's powers, despite it happening so many times before. Why not now?"

"Why not? Because I'm fucking hungry and tired. That's why."

Thumbing toward her, Tor said to Luca, "She does have a point."

Luca narrowed his eyes at both of them, then focused on Tor. "Don't think you're gonna get out of this. I'm getting to the bottom of your powers if it's the last thing I do."

"Oh, for fuck's sake…" Frida's eyes gave off a soft yellow glow. She tore off her feathered bolero and tossed it at him. The bolero morphed into a coil of black rope that bound Luca's arms, torso, and legs.

"Ack!" Luca squirmed futilely against the bound constraint. "What'd I do?"

Frida stepped toward him. "No more talk about tonight. No more obsessing over Tor's powers. We're going to our suite now. Got it?" She prodded him in the chest.

Luca slouched and gave her a slow, compliant nod.

The glow in Frida's eyes disappeared, and she glared at Tor. "I'm keeping the trailer key until we get back home, and that's final."

"Yes, ma'am!" Tor said with a mock salute.

Frida headed for the hotel's entrance, and Tor followed, with the bound Luca hefted over his shoulder. As they walked, Tor heard the snobbish rumblings of passersby, who cast the three of them condescending glances. Tor ignored their complaints of "drunken convicts" and "troublemakers" and headed to the elevator. One of the desk clerks watched them then picked up the phone, but one of her colleagues stopped her, whispering something into her ear. Her face flushing slightly, the clerk returned the phone receiver to the cradle.

Rarely was Tor away from his beloved Myollnir, but when he was, he'd made sure it was secured under lock and key. Sometimes he wondered if his obsession was part of the source of his losing control. Tor considered what Luca had said earlier. Maybe it was about time he really learned about his powers—and how to control them.

Myollnir was the last gift Tor had received from Brock Olsson, who'd first taught Tor how to play the guitar, before he died in a car crash. Brock had been one of his closest friends and mentor, and Tor would never forgive himself if something happened to the guitar.

"All right, c'mon. Can you *pleeease* untie me? I promise to be good," Luca whined once they stepped off the elevator onto the ninth floor. "This is really embarrassing being carried by Tor like a caveman's wife. And my balls are being crushed on his shoulder."

Tor and Frida exchanged amused glances. Then Frida's eyes gave off a golden glow, and the rope holding Luca morphed back into a feathered bolero, releasing him. The bolero floated to Frida and returned to her shoulders. Tor set Luca on his feet.

Luca stumbled, remaining hunched over, then braced himself against Tor. "Ugh. Thanks, Frida. I may never have kids now."

"Awesome. I can barely stand having *one* of you around."

Tor laughed and continued down the hall. As he drew closer to their suite, the door opened. Two men dressed in white button-down shirts, black pants, and matching black bow ties rolled an empty metal cart out of the room and started down the hall. The door shut behind them.

"Who are those guys?" Frida whispered.

The men nodded as Tor and his friends stepped aside to let them pass. As the men walked by, Tor noticed the hotel's tree logo on one of their name badges.

"Room service," Tor figured.

"But we didn't order room service," Frida said.

Tor shrugged. "Maybe they were cleaning the room?"

"In black bow ties?"

"Have you forgotten where we are? The cleaning crew probably scrub the toilets wearing three-piece suits and diamond-studded rubber gloves."

"Why are you complaining, Fri?" Luca said. "Maybe they were delivering a big cake, since, you know, the owner idolizes us?"

"We *have* been pampered like royalty here," Tor agreed. "I'm really gonna miss sleeping on beds this soft and comfortable."

"Dude, I still can't figure out which one of those zillion knobs turns on the shower!"

Frida arched an eyebrow. "You actually remembered to shower? Ragnarok is upon us…"

Tor opened the door. A delectable whiff of cooked meats suddenly filled his nostrils. Sitting on a long white-clothed table in the middle of the great room were nine polished-steel cloches set in a neat line. Next to the table sat a kegerator on wheels, with three frosted mugs on top. His jaw dropped.

"Holy shit!" Frida said.

"That's an understatement," Luca said.

"There's beer!" Tor made a beeline for the kegerator and filled up a frosted mug. The contents smelled of Warrior's Stout. As he brought the mug to his lips, he paused and narrowed his eyes at Luca. "Wait, this isn't another one of your tricks, is it?"

Luca shook his head. "I didn't do this." He approached and lifted one of the cloches. Beneath the escaped cloud of steam was a plate piled high with chopped steak. He blinked. "Oh, man. This couldn't be any more real!" He uncovered the rest: hearty soups, fresh salads, smothered pork chops, rice, mixed vegetables, and an assortment of desserts.

Tor's hunger was curbed only by his desire for beer. It had been a long, stressful night, and he needed something to calm his nerves. As the edge of the frosted mug touched his lips, Frida snatched it away, sloshing brown liquid over the edge.

"Stop. We didn't order room service. Aren't you the least bit suspicious as to why they were here?"

Tor eyed the mug in her hands and frowned. She wasn't likely to surrender it willingly, so he grabbed another mug, filled it, and took a few steps away from her, out of her reach. "Maybe it was Harold." He gulped half its contents. The wonderful honey-infused taste teased his taste buds, and his cheeks hurt from smiling so wide. "It's gotta be Harold."

Frida made a face. "Why would Harold do all this, after what happened tonight?"

Tor gulped the rest and helped himself to a refill. "I told you, he doesn't know."

"Bullshit. He probably knew before it happened."

"Maybe, for once, the old man's powers are getting rusty," Luca said, cutting a slice of strawberry cheesecake. "He's been a good manager to us. We smashed it tonight and got free food. What more can you ask for, Fri?"

"First of all, he's not that old. Second, don't you think he would've said something about this beforehand?"

Luca settled on the chaise lounge with his plate. "Maybe he wanted to surprise us for a job well done."

"Fuck this. I'm calling him." She took out her phone and punched in Harold's number. Moments later, she swore under her breath and ended the call. "Of course, it goes straight to voicemail."

"Great. Maybe he's getting us more work," Luca said.

A knock came at the door. Tor ignored it in favor of his third refill, while Luca shoveled another giant forkful of cheesecake in his mouth.

"Oh, please, don't get up," Frida scoffed. She went to the front door and peered through the peephole. She looked back at Tor and Luca with raised eyebrows as she undid the locks. She opened the door, and Devin Stevenson, the hotel's owner, stood in the doorway in a hunter-green polo shirt, the hotel's gold-embroidered tree logo emblazoned over his heart, and crisp black pants. A rolled-up white cloth was clenched in his hand. His slicked-back sandy-blond hair revealed the handsome features of his clean-shaven, young face as he grinned widely at Frida.

"Wow, Ms. Winters, how are you?"

Frida returned the smile. "I'm good, thanks. By the way, just Frida's fine."

"Okay… Frida." Devin nodded then craned his neck, peering past her toward Tor and Luca. "The staff said they saw you guys come in. Looks like I timed the caterers just right."

Tor met Devin's gaze then furrowed his brow. "You did all this for us?"

Devin beamed. "Of course! It's complimentary. It's the least I can do, having the greatest Viking metal band of all time staying at my hotel. What an honor!"

Luca swallowed the last of his cake and licked the icing off his fingers. "Who are we to say no to our diehard fans?"

"I heard through the grapevine what happened to you guys tonight at the Death by Metal event.

Man, if I hadn't had this high-profile wedding tonight, I would've been there, front and center to experience your awesomeness."

Tor made a face. "Experience what? Us getting kicked out?"

"No, listening to you guys perform. I heard it was sick. And you, Tor, letting loose on stage like that to the point you just destroy things? I'd live for that moment, feeling that energy and emotion you put into your songs." He shook his fist for emphasis. "That's why you guys are amazing."

Frida snorted.

Luca crossed his arms and smirked at Tor, giving him an "I told you so" look.

Devin unfurled the white cloth in his hand, revealing a large T-shirt with VanAseir's logo—the symbol of three interlocked triangles, the *valknut*—printed on the front. "Before I go, can you sign this? It's for my teenaged daughter. She's really into you guys, too." He pulled a fat black marker from his pocket.

"An autograph? You bet!" Luca bounded over to Devin, swiped the marker, and happily scrawled his name across the front.

Tor knew VanAesir had fans, but he had no idea their fans existed this far out of Seattle. All the band had was one small online fan page. Most of their popularity came from word of mouth among the Seattle-Tacoma locals. One blown amp was nothing compared to how much their music reached their fans like Devin and his daughter.

"Thanks so much! You guys rock!" Devin said after Tor and Frida signed their names. "All right, I know you all had a long night, so I'll be on my way." He headed for the door then paused. "By the way, can I get you guys anything else? Anything at all?"

Frida shook her head. "No, tha—"

"Can you bring another one of those up?" Tor pointed to the kegerator, ignoring Frida's glare. "That one's definitely not gonna last too much longer."

Devin beamed from ear to ear. "Can I! When I heard you were going to be staying here, I made sure there was enough Warrior's Stout on hand. I'll tell the staff to bring another one up right away." He left with a happy pep in his step.

Frida reset the locks and exhaled. "Damn it, Tor. We better not be overstaying our welcome with your demands."

Tor shrugged. "What demands? He got us free food! He even bought Warrior's Stout just for me!

Can you believe it? This guy treats us like kings… uh, and queens."

"Hey, I'm not complaining about that," Luca said, refilling his plate with more desserts. "He's a diehard fan who appreciates our music."

"He's also running a business," Frida explained. "He may have given us free food, but I doubt the beer is endless. He probably thinks we're loaded or something. Harold will have our asses if we run up the hotel bill."

"All right, fine. I won't bother Devin anymore." Tor rolled his eyes. He decided to finally check out the spread for himself. Devin's visit had eased Tor's stress of the sour night enough to rejuvenate his appetite. He piled his plate high with some of everything and retreated to a comfortable chair near the kegerator.

The food was cooked to perfection, much to Tor's delight. Knowing he wouldn't eat this good for a while, he ate until he was stuffed.

Another knock came at the door shortly after. Tor perked, anticipating the kegerator delivery, but Frida's words tugged the back of his mind. He hated to have to refuse his favorite beer, but if it meant sparing Harold's wrath, he would do it.

Frida set her empty plate aside, hopped up from the couch, and headed to the door. After a quick check through the peephole, she scrambled for the locks and flung open the door. Harold stood in the doorway, dressed in his usual, finely pressed grey business suit, a tan briefcase tucked under one arm.

His salt-and-pepper hair neatly trimmed, he inclined his head to her. A smile appeared beneath his matching shadow of beard. "Frida."

"Hey, Harold." Frida let him in and gestured toward the great room.

Luca gobbled a slice of chocolate cake faster than Tor could blink. "Harold! Dude, the hotel owner came by earlier and gave us this humongous spread!"

"Devin?" Harold's brow furrowed. "Huh. I told him what time you guys were returning to the hotel, but I didn't think he'd do all this." He pinned the three of them with a hard stare. "Be very grateful Devin loves you guys so much."

"See? Someone who appreciates Tor going berserk on stage." Luca grinned and nodded.

Harold shook his head. "More like he's a fan of your music, not your performance."

Tor looked sidelong at Harold from across the room before turning away to refill his beer. Though his belly was full, he could always make room for Warrior's Stout. Its high alcohol content was not for the faint of heart, but his body's natural fortitude—the same one that kept him from electrocuting himself every time he used his powers—also gave him a superhuman tolerance for alcohol. As a result, he could drink as much as he wanted without the side effects.

Harold settled on the couch and clicked opened his briefcase. He pulled out two small envelopes. "Here. Think of these as a small bonus. You guys continue to impress." He held out envelopes to Luca and Frida.

Frida approached and took hers. On his way back to get the last slice of chocolate cake, Luca swiped up his envelope. Tor continued drinking, not knowing—and pretending not to care—if there was an envelope waiting for him. But sensing the small niggling feeling in his mind, he figured not to get his hopes up.

"Well? Aren't you going to open them?" Harold raised his eyebrows.

Frida stared at the envelope a moment, swallowed, and tore it open. Inside was a yellow slip of paper. "A deposit receipt for five hundred bucks?"

"Sweet! I got one, too!" Luca held up the paper, grinning wide.

Harold adjusted his glasses and nodded. "It's all been credited to your accounts. Just a little something from Jayce, the head coordinator at the Death by Metal event."

Frida blinked. "What? Jayce still paid us, despite what happened?"

"I already knew what was going to happen, which was why I requested prepayment for just the two of you." Harold nodded to Luca and Frida. Then his light-brown eyes cut to Tor, and they narrowed.

Tor paused mid gulp. *Damn. He knew.*

"You're lucky my foresight spans a day, or else we'd be financially in deep shit right now," Harold said.

"So if you already knew, why did you ask me about the payment?" Tor spat.

"I wanted to see if you'd come clean. But apparently, you can't even trust your manager. I already told Jayce to withhold your cut of the profit long before your performance."

"I didn't tell you because I didn't want you to blow up on me like you always do whenever I tell the truth," Tor muttered, looking away. "I'm tired of everyone blowing up on me!"

"Then stop blowing up the damned stage!" Frida said.

Tor caught Frida's hard stare, and he sighed. "Look, I'm trying my hardest to stay in control."

"Not hard enough, it seems." Harold shook his head.

Tor attempted to refill his mug, but discovered the kegerator was finally tapped out. Growling, he slammed the empty mug onto the table. "Damn it!"

Harold pinned Tor with a glare. "Oh yeah, I told the staff *not* to deliver any more kegerators to this room. What are you trying to do? Make us all go bankrupt from your bottomless stomach?"

Tor scowled. "How was I supposed to know it wasn't complimentary with the rest of the food?"

"Devin's a businessman, first and foremost. People tend to assume musicians and entertainers have money to burn, and they'll latch onto that opportunity—and your wallet—and suck you dry. Don't trust everyone you meet, Tor. That's the basic number-one rule of navigating the music world."

"Hey, give Tor a break," Luca said. "Everyone loves him. The crowd loved every minute of his performance. They wanted more. Even Devin couldn't stop talking about our music. His daughter loves us, too!"

Harold took off his glasses and rubbed one of the lenses on his sleeve. "Gods help me, now I know why the guys at the agency were quick to assign this band to me," he grumbled, resetting his glasses. "Look, Tor. That kind of performance isn't financially viable. The more this happens, the less venues you'll be invited to. You're lucky I managed to get you guys into Valhalla Injection. Don't screw this up."

"What am I supposed to do?" Tor blurted, his hands balling into fists. His heart pounded, and he felt small static shocks ripple through his hands. "I put my heart and soul into these songs! I do it not just for me, or this band, but for Brock. He would've wanted me to give it my best all the time. And damn it, I will. I'm not gonna do this half-assed just to keep my powers in control."

"No one's telling you to do anything half-assed. But your powers are undoubtedly a liability, and something needs to be done about them, and I mean *before* you guys perform at Valhalla Injection. If you screw this up, you can kiss your music careers goodbye."

"We don't have much time to get our shit together," Frida muttered.

"Say, Harold," Luca said. "Can you see what'll happen at Valhalla Injection? Are we gonna kill it again?"

Harold rolled his eyes. "Even if I could see that far into the future, I wouldn't tell you that. Regardless, what you all do now will determine the outcome."

"Which means we should get practicing," Luca said.

"No, tonight we take a break and get ready to head back to Seattle," Frida said.

"Listen to the lady." Harold thumbed at Frida then got up from the couch. "Get some rest, you three. We've a long trip ahead of us. Be ready tomorrow by nine a.m." He left, the door slamming behind him.

Annoyed, Tor stormed to his private bedroom. He lay in bed and stared at the ceiling, his mind jumbled with thoughts. If he took his uncontrollable powers to Valhalla Injection, the band's future was shot. They had five days to get their act together. No doubt the other Seattle bands, including their archrivals Jotnar Malice, were already ahead in their preparations. He clenched his jaw. He wouldn't be surprised if Tristan found a way to get his band into Valhalla Injection. Tristan was always trying to one-up him. What better way than to knock it out of the park at one of the largest Viking death metal events on the West Coast?

But if Tor couldn't even control himself, he doubted he would be able to help his band go far. Valhalla Injection might very well mean the death of VanAesir.

CHAPTER FOUR

Here we are," Tristan said.

Zeke muttered under his breath as he turned into the entrance of the World Tree Hotel's massive parking lot. "How did those bastards end up in this snazzy place?"

"Who cares?" Tristan said. "Myollnir is here."

Zeke's stomach rumbled. "And I'm still hungry."

"Shut up about food," Scarlet growled from the backseat.

As they did a few laps around the brightly lit, filled lot, Tristan scanned the sea of cars. VanAesir's trailer was nowhere to be found. "Maybe they're parked in the back," he finally said.

Zeke sighed and turned a corner, making his way to the farthest lot. At almost three in the morning, the back lot was devoid of people. Among the larger vehicles was VanAesir's black SUV and trailer with the band's *valknut* logo emblazoned on the sides.

"There!" Tristan pointed.

Zeke parked in a nearby empty space. "All right, so go get Myollnir."

"Easier said than done." Dahlia pointed out the slow-roaming orange-yellow lights of a security guard's car threading its way through the lot.

Scarlet opened the passenger door. "I'll keep an eye on the guard and make sure he doesn't get too close. Meet you guys outside the parking lot exit." She blew a flirty kiss at them and casually walked off, weaving her way through the lot.

"Heads up." Eric pointed to a light post in front of them. Near the top, a tiny red dot from a security camera blinked steadily.

Tristan grumbled under his breath. "Dahlia, deal with that camera."

"The electromagnetic interference can't be maintained for too long, or we'll risk being discovered," Dahlia warned. "Get Myollnir, and get it fast."

"Yeah, yeah. You just do your part."

Dahlia got out the van and walked around the light post. Standing out of the camera's sight range, she raised her hands. A subtle white glow emitted from them then disappeared. Faint electric sparks crackled around the camera as if it had blown a fuse. Its red light flickered erratically.

Time to go. Tristan looked to the driver's seat. "Keep the engine running and be ready."

Zeke sighed and stared ahead out the windshield. "Yeah, sure."

Tristan turned to the backseat, where Eric sat holding his head, as if in pain. "Damn it, don't crap out on me now. I need you with me to watch my back."

Eric groaned. "Ugh, my brain feels like it's gonna explode. I keep telling Dahlia to warn me first before she does her damned EMI…"

Tristan frowned. Eric's gift of sharp hearing, which was far keener than a dog's, didn't come without a price. His hypersensitivity to certain electromagnetic frequencies gave him constant migraines, especially when Dahlia used her powers near him.

Tristan hopped out of the camper van. "Come on, Eric. Stay with me here. We don't have much time."

His hand still splayed over his forehead, Eric stumbled out of the backseat and followed Tristan.

"Hold on…" Eric whispered.

Tristan looked over his shoulder. Eric still rubbed his head, the pained look on his face not quite as severe since they were farther away from Dahlia. "What now?"

"Trying to tune some shit out…" Eric winced, rubbed his ear, and looked toward the distant orange-yellow lights, which had stopped their free roaming. The pained expression lessened, and his face brightened. His ears twitched, and he smiled. "Sounds like that security guard's a Jotnar Malice fan."

"What?"

"I heard him tell Scarlet that he has all of our albums." Eric's grin widened. "I think tonight's working out to be in our favor."

"Fuck yeah." Tristan stopped in front of the trailer's back door, which was secured with a large metal combination padlock. He snorted.

Eric stood by, shifting his weight in an anxious twitch. "Dahlia said to hurry up. And I hear people in the hotel talking about the malfunctioning camera. Security's been alerted."

Grasping the padlock firmly, Tristan concentrated, tapping deep into his inner strength. His brain numbed as his body responded to his power's calling. A burst of adrenaline surged through his veins. The muscles in his arms cramped as they became firmer and stronger. With a quick clench of his fist, he yanked the metal lock from the door and crumpled it like paper. He pitched the damaged lock into some nearby bushes then unlatched and opened the trailer door. He pulled his cell phone from his pocket, activated the flashlight, and scanned through the instrument cases and equipment.

"We need to get out of here. *Now*," Eric said.

"Not without my prize," Tristan said, stepping inside the trailer and rummaging through the items. He uncovered a guitar case secured with another, more complicated-looking padlock and covered in stickers of various Nordic runes, pin-up girls, and the band's logo. As he grabbed the case's handle, he felt the hairs on his arm rise from static electricity. He grinned. "This is it. Let's go." He tried to lift the case and nearly threw his arm out when the case wouldn't budge. "Shit!"

"What's wrong now?" Eric asked, peering inside the trailer.

"Nothing, I'm fine," Tristan grumbled, summoning his strength once more. He huffed, barely managing to lift the case. *How the fuck does Tor play this thing?*

"Need help?"

"No!" Tristan grunted, concentrating harder, his subconscious grasping the very core of his strength. Gritting his teeth, he lifted the case, the veins in his arm visibly straining. He huffed, leaving the trailer with the case that felt heavier than a boulder.

Eric shut and relatched the trailer door. He helped Tristan carry the case as they hurried back to the camper van, where Dahlia and Zeke were waiting, Tristan climbed into the passenger's seat, clutching Myollnir's case in his arms. He released his power and wiped a layer of sweat from his brow, his mind momentarily blanking out from the sudden shut-off of adrenaline.

"Drive," Tristan ordered.

Grumbling, Zeke drove off toward the parking lot's rear exit.

"I hope you got what you needed, 'cause I'm done," Dahlia huffed.

Tristan sighed and shifted comfortably in his seat. "Tonight was a good night."

They left the lot, picking up Scarlet along the way. During the return trip to the campground where they were staying temporarily, they grabbed a couple of pies from a twenty-four-hour pizza joint.

"Contact everyone you know and tell them to come to the party this Friday night," Tristan told his friends.

Scarlet wolfed down her pizza slice. "What party?"

"The one we'll be throwing at the Giant's Tap as a pre-victory celebration of winning Battle of the Bands at Valhalla Injection."

Scarlet's face lit up with fiery fervor. "You're that confident we'll win?"

Tristan patted the guitar case. "We've got Myollnir now. Nothing can stop us from winning."

"VanAesir will be out of the game. That's for sure," Eric said. "They were our biggest competition. I dare say bigger than Stingray Armageddon."

Tristan shook his head. "Not anymore."

Zeke grabbed the last slice. "Things are gonna be different when we get back to Seattle."

"I can't wait!" Scarlet said.

"I could use some sleep first," Dahlia said, opening the side door. Cool, crisp air rushed inside, overtaking the van's strong pizza smell.

"Where are you going?" Scarlet asked.

"I don't get to sleep under *that* too often in the city," Dahlia replied, gesturing to the clear starry sky and bright moon.

"Mmm. I think I'll join you." Scarlet shoved empty pizza boxes aside and climbed out of the van.

"We're hitting the road at dawn," Tristan told them. "The sooner we get back, the better."

"We'll be ready, little brother," Scarlet called back.

After the women left, Eric and Zeke settled into their respective sleeping areas in the camper. Tristan reclined in his seat, one arm draped around the guitar case. His arm tingled from the pulsing waves of static electricity that seemed to flow from the case. It was an odd, yet satisfying feeling to know that such power to influence millions was contained within. *Once I master you, Jotnar Malice will be a household name, and VanAesir will be nothing but a memory.*

Chapter Five

Despite the sleeping tablet he'd taken before going to bed, Tor had barely gotten any sleep—his reoccurring dreams kept replaying in his mind, getting more frightening each time. The single giant from his mythical dream world had somehow multiplied to five. It was no longer Myollnir that drew them, but something else. Something seemingly far more powerful than Tor could fathom.

Tor fought the faceless beings endlessly but could not conquer them. Each time the battles replayed in his dream, his brutal losses were more gruesome. When he finally saw himself lying on the ground in a pool of his own blood, Tor sprang awake from the nightmare. His heart pounding furiously, he stared at his slick, sweaty hands. The hairs on his arms stood ramrod straight as electric pangs of adrenaline flowed through his veins. Tor stared out the window at the morning sun rising above the horizon, painting the clear skies in a warm, serene orange. Examining his hands again, long and hard, he thought about his dream. *What did all that mean?*

After showering and getting dressed, Tor packed up his large duffel bag and hauled it down to the trailer. His friends couldn't complain to him this time that he wasn't ready to leave at once. While he loved staying at the glamorous World Tree Hotel, he preferred the simple three-bedroom apartment he shared with Frida and Luca.

As he approached the trailer, he sensed something was wrong. Something was… missing. The subtle electric pulse—a constant reminder of his strong connection with Myollnir—no longer thrummed in the back of his mind. The tips of his fingers tingled with faint sparks of weakened energy then fizzled to numbness. Cringing, Tor flexed his fingers in an attempt to revitalize the nerves. *Damn, that nightmare fucked with my head worse than I thought...*

He rounded the back of the trailer and stopped. The door was shut, but the padlock was gone. Tor's breath hitched. He dropped his duffel bag and flung open the trailer door. Luca's drums, Frida's bass, and the other equipment were all there, still intact. *But where's Myollnir?*

His ears rang. He took a breath, and his lungs constricted. He gasped for air and braced himself on the edge of the trailer while he waited for his body to catch up with his mind. *It's probably buried under all this stuff. That's all,* he tried to convince himself as he turned the trailer upside down. He unloaded every item from the trailer and SUV into the parking lot then packed them again.

He stared blankly at the items stuffed back into the trailer haphazardly. Myollnir was gone.

* * *

Luca sat up in bed and yawned, stretching. It had been a crazy, amazing, fun night. And he'd slept great, too. He was going to miss living like a king. Once they returned to Seattle, it would be back to the harsh reality of sharing an apartment with his friends.

After getting dressed, Luca packed up his things, left his room, and headed to the kitchen to make coffee. He noticed Tor's bedroom door was open, and Tor was gone.

Probably went for a walk. There was no ignoring Tor's edginess last night. Not even the endless amount of Warrior's Stout Tor had drank seemed to calm his nerves.

Waiting for the coffee to finish brewing, Luca peered out the large window at the ominous dark clouds that swirled over the city. *Weird... wasn't it just sunny and clear earlier?*

A series of pounding footsteps echoed through the hallway outside the suite, interrupting Luca's thoughts. The suite's front door suddenly burst open.

Frantic with rage, Tor bounded in. "Myollnir's gone!" he exclaimed, his eyes as wide as saucers.

Luca casually poured some coffee in a mug. "Good morning to you, too, sunshine," he said in a calm, yet amused tone. "Myollnir's gone? Did you have another bad dream?" He said it jokingly, knowing full well no one could ever pick up the guitar's case, much less steal it.

Tor's jaw tightened, and the veins in his forearms pulsed. "I'm serious, Luca."

The edge of the mug halted at Luca's lips. "Are you sure?"

"Am I sure? Why the fuck would I be making it up?"

Luca set the mug down. "Let's go down and check."

"I've checked and checked. I don't sense Myollnir anywhere. I'm telling you—it's gone."

Luca wanted to remain optimistic that Tor's guitar hadn't gone far, for both his and Frida's sake. It was bad enough that Tor had a hard time controlling his powers, constantly ready to explode like a ticking lightning bomb. It would be a disaster if he were any more stressed out. "Look, you're obviously worked up. Maybe you just missed it," he said, heading for the front door. "I'll go with you, and we can look together. There's no way it's just *gone.*"

Luca marched outside to the parking lot with Tor hot on his heels. The air felt tense and stiff, and the faint smell of ozone filled Luca's nose. The hairs on his arm stood on end, tickling his skin. He looked up and noticed the ominous clouds were getting thicker, covering the sky in a dreary black.

Odd, he thought, rounding to the back of the trailer. He halted. Noting the missing padlock, he unlatched and opened the trailer. The once-neatly-packed equipment was in disarray.

"I see you've done a thorough search," Luca said sourly.

"Look, we're wasting our time here," Tor said.

Something glinted out of the corner of Luca's eye, and he paused. The dim, morning light reflected off a small shiny object in the bushes nearby. "Time reveals all, Tor," he said, approaching the cluster of foliage and plucking out the mysterious object. A wad of crushed metal sat in his palm. Luca noted the remnants of a familiar number dial and frowned. "This was no ordinary robbery," he said, showing Tor the crumpled lock.

Tor swiped it from Luca's hands, examined it a moment, then studied the back of the trailer.

Luca grabbed the object back. "This is a five-hundred-dollar lock, crushed like a paper wad." He tried to enclose the metal ball in his hand, but the sharp edges sliced his palm. He winced. "This was done by someone or some*thing.*"

"Strength of a giant, like in my dream," Tor muttered, his face blank. Then his eyes went wide. "Shit!" Sparks of electricity crackled in his eyes.

Luca opened his mouth, about to ask Tor what he was mumbling about, when a bolt of lightning suddenly speared from the sky, striking the lightning rod atop the hotel's roof. A shower of sparks rained down. A loud rumble of thunder followed, shaking the ground and tripping alarms on several cars in the parking lot.

Luca jumped. "Whoa! That sounded close!"

Tor marched back to the hotel without another word. Another bolt of lightning struck nearby, causing the lights in the parking lot to flicker briefly. Thunder crackled and boomed, its resonance causing another minor quake.

Luca watched him and shivered. If destruction happened when Tor got caught up in his music, what kind of chaos was his anger going to unleash?

* * *

Tor could barely breathe, his mind constantly stressing over the loss of his beloved Myollnir. *It's gotta be Tristan...* he thought, storming through the hotel lobby. He would have preferred the culprit was some rabid fan who happened to possess super strength, but the deep-seated rivalry between Tristan and Tor made it obvious.

Tor approached the front desk. A uniformed woman typed steadily on an unseen computer with one hand while holding a steaming coffee mug with the other. She stopped typing, looked up, and smiled.

"Good morning, Mr. Hagen! How may I help you?" the woman asked cheerily.

Tor slammed his fist on the counter, cracking the granite and sending electric sparks trailing through the tiny fissures before fizzling out. The lights in the lobby dimmed and flickered as thunder echoed outside.

The woman jumped with a yelp, dropping the mug. It crashed to the floor with a spluttering crack. "S-sir, is everything okay?" she asked in a quivering voice.

Tor gritted his teeth. "My guitar was stolen last night. Is Tristan Westgard staying at this hotel?"

The receptionist blinked then looked at the computer screen. "Ah, I-I don't recall seeing that name. Let me check…" She typed on the keyboard with shaky fingers.

Tor white-knuckled the edge of the counter as he waited, his patience wearing thin. Once Tor located Tristan, he would make him pay. Someone slapped him on the shoulder, jerking him out of his thoughts. He looked sideways.

"Tor, quit harassing the receptionist." Harold glared. "Luca found your guitar." He gestured to Luca, who stood behind him with Myollnir's case loaded onto a luggage cart. Luca shrugged at Tor, his face scrunched in trepidation.

Tor stared open-mouthed. "Myollnir!" He still couldn't feel its pulsating energy, though. Perhaps he'd been apart from it long enough to affect their connection. Or maybe his emotions were clouding his judgment. "Wait, where did you—"

Harold held up a hand. "Let's take this upstairs. I think we've disturbed this poor receptionist enough."

The woman swallowed. Her gaze bounced nervously from Tor to Harold. "It-It's all right. R-Really! I'm glad Mr. Hagen's guitar was found."

Tor approached the luggage cart, but Harold stuck his arm out, stopping him.

"Not so fast. You need to calm down first. We'll deal with this *upstairs,*" Harold said, his glaring eyes giving off a faint, golden glow that sent a chill down Tor's spine.

Tor swallowed. Clenching both fists, he took a final glance at Myollnir sitting on the luggage cart, spun around, and marched toward the elevators.

Back in the suite, Tor discovered Frida sprawled on the couch, engrossed in her phone. She was fully dressed, her kinky golden hair twisted out in a wild style. Sitting at her feet was her packed cat-printed weekender bag. She glanced at Tor, Luca, and Harold then resumed texting.

The front door slammed shut. Tor spun around and reached Luca in a few strides. "All right. I'm fine, now. Give me my guitar."

Luca cringed. "Uh…" He scratched the back of his head.

Tor shoved Luca out of the way. He grabbed the handle to Myollnir's case and lifted it from the luggage cart. The image of the guitar case suddenly morphed into his duffel bag.

Tor blinked. Electric rage surged through his veins. He slammed down the duffel bag and grabbed Luca's shirt with both hands. "You think this is some kind of joke?" Tor growled, tightening his grip on Luca's shirt. Thunder roared outside, shaking the suite.

"Harold made me do it!" Luca blurted, putting his hands up in surrender.

Tor narrowed his eyes then released Luca with a hard shove. He turned to Harold. "Are you serious right now? Myollnir's been stolen, and you pull this shit?"

Harold folded his arms across his chest and shook his head slowly.

"Wait, what? Myollnir was *stolen*?" Frida asked.

Tor met her concerned gaze and nodded. "Yeah, and I'm pretty sure it was Tristan's doing, that bastard."

Frida's eyebrows rose. "Seriously? I mean, I knew he was strong, but I didn't think anyone could actually budge that case."

"He's obviously stronger than we thought," Tor said. *Like the giants in my dream…* He shuddered at the thought then whipped his head back to Harold. "Apparently Harold and Luca thought it would be funny to fuck with me."

"I told you he made me do it!" Luca whined.

"Enough!" Harold barked at them. "Yes, Tor, I told Luca to make the illusion so that you'd calm down while we figured out a plan to get it back."

Tor shook his head. "There's no plan to figure out. Tristan has it. I'm certain. And I'm going to find him."

"Look, Tor," Harold explained. "Tristan and the rest of Jotnar Malice are probably already en route back to Seattle to get ready for Valhalla Injection—exactly what we must do."

Frowning, Luca nudged Harold in the arm. "You know, you could've just warned us about this beforehand."

Harold rolled his eyes. "First of all, I don't keep track of every damned thing in the world twenty-four seven. I am limited to focusing on one person, place, or thing at a time, and even then, it is only when I choose to use my foresight. Believe me, Luca. This power is *not* something you want to abuse."

Tor paced back and forth, combing his fingers through his hair. His head pounded from stress. He stopped in front of the large window and stared blankly at the buildings beneath the overcast sky. He exhaled. *I'm sorry, Brock. I let you down...*

"I hate to say it, but..." Luca began, "I was wondering how long it would take Tristan to finally do this."

Tor perked. "What!" Gritting his teeth, he snapped his gaze to Luca then stormed over to the chair, where Luca was perched on the armrest. "You anticipated this all along?"

Luca jumped, nearly falling off the armrest, but caught himself with awkward grace. "Uh, s-sort of, but…" He found his new perch on the edge of the couch's armrest, far enough from Tor's reach. "I didn't think he'd have enough balls to steal it right out of our trailer."

Frida's eyes narrowed, and she scooted closer to him on the couch. "Explain."

Luca hopped up from the armrest and backed away slowly, until he bumped into Harold, who stood like a statue with his arms crossed, his dark eyes bearing down on him. Luca cleared his throat, and his eyes darted between the three of them. "Er… I've been noticing for a while now, that certain look in Tristan's eye every time he'd watched Tor perform. One day, I'd overheard Tristan talking to the other Jotnar Malice members, coming up with some plan to steal Tor's guitar, or at least get rid of it.

"He believed if Tor didn't have Myollnir, he'd give up on playing, which would allow the other local bands—namely Jotnar Malice—the opportunity to rise in the city. But I guess they couldn't agree on a solid plan, so Tristan gave up— at least I thought he did."

Tor clenched and unclenched his fists. "If he stole my guitar, then that might also mean he can play it. That bastard knows what he's doing."

Luca shrugged. "I doubt he can play it. I mean, the way its crafted is so unorthodox for such a common type of instrument. It really takes a special skill to produce a tune on that thing."

"Since when has that ever stopped someone like Tristan?" Tor asked.

"Yeah, well. I bet it'll be a bitch for him to try and learn the secrets of Myollnir in only a few days' time. I think in his case, he just wants to eliminate the competition. Every musician has their preferred instrument, and he took yours away. But we'll get it back, somehow."

Frida snorted. "You know, part of me was kind of glad Myollnir was gone. Can you imagine? We might actually manage to get through our entire set without Tor destroying something."

Tor gave her a sour look.

"That might be a bit of a stretch," Harold said, rubbing his chin contemplatively.

"Without Myollnir, we'd lose our edge on stage and kiss our chances of winning Battle of the Bands goodbye," Luca said.

"You guys act like Myollnir is the only reason why our band is so great and popular," Tor interjected. "You heard Devin. He likes the passion we put in our songs. It's us who's great. We've got the sound and passion that our fans love. But playing Myollnir just helps me channel my own passion. I can't imagine ever playing another. That guitar means more to me than just music. It's a reminder of one of the greatest friends I ever had and lost. And all of the great friends and family I've had since. I play it for them. I play it for you guys. I play it for myself."

Frida inclined her head. "I know how much it means to you, Tor. I just get annoyed when you get obsessive or when you lose control of your powers because of it."

"Take the good with the bad, Fri," Luca said with a small smile. "We may not be able to get through a set, but our fans will still love us."

The corner of Frida's lips tugged upward. "Yeah… I guess you're right. I'll admit, being a part of this band has been one of the most interesting experiences of my music career."

Tor smiled slightly at her. A hint of relief spread through him as Frida's words repeated in his mind.

Did that mean she was having second thoughts about leaving?

As if Frida could read his mind, her faint smile disappeared. "But there needs to come a point where we as a band actually move forward in our career. We can't keep up this same old shit. I can't stay in a band like that. I have a life, too. A career I want to see improved."

A lump formed in the back of Tor's throat. She seemed more certain about what she wanted to do with her life, and she was still on the fence about VanAesir—an even greater reason why he needed to find Myollnir as soon as he could.

"You need to learn how to control yourself first, Tor," Harold said. "Finding Myollnir will mean nothing until you've done that."

"I'm working on it," Tor muttered, turning back to the window. A streak of lightning flashed across the sky, followed by a distant rumble of thunder.

"Seriously, what is up with the crazy weather?" Frida said, joining Tor by the window.

"It's just a thunderstorm," Tor said.

Frida turned her head. "A thunderstorm? In LA?"

Tor shrugged.

"Is this another one of your doing?"

"Why would it be my doing? I don't control the weather."

"Because you and electricity go hand in hand."

Tor rolled his eyes. "There are millions of people in LA. I'm sure I'm not the only one with an affinity for electricity."

Harold muttered under his breath. "Let's pack up and hit the road before there are any more anomalies."

Luca cringed. "Ugh, seventeen hours trapped in an SUV with Tor this moody? Gods, help us all…"

CHAPTER SIX

Tor stared out the window at the rolling dark clouds and endless streaks of lightning. *Myollnir.* He clenched and unclenched his fists. Fat drops of rain pelted the window, obscuring his view.

"Will this storm ever let up?" Luca grumbled. "We've been driving in it for hours."

Tearing his gaze from the window, Tor looked sidelong at his friend.

Harold sighed. "It's probably best that we stop and wait it out. We need to fill up anyway."

Luca's stomach growled. "Yeah, I could sure use a fill-up."

When they arrived at a service station in Sacramento, Tor hopped out of the SUV while Harold began fueling it up. Frida and Luca headed into the convenience store, and Tor walked around the front of the SUV. He leaned against the hood, crossing his arms. As he watched the pouring rain beyond the station's metal canopy, his mind raced again. *What if Tristan is unable to play Myollnir and manages to destroy it out of frustration?* He clenched his jaw. *Damn it.* Brock had taken Myollnir's crafting design to the grave—such an elusive instrument could never be duplicated.

"Dude, look what they had!"

"Huh?" Tor blinked out of his thoughts.

Luca and Frida approached with bags in tow. Grinning, Luca pulled out a bottle of Warrior's Stout from one of the bags. "Just what you need, eh?"

Tor frowned and stared back at the rain. "Thanks, but I'm not thirsty."

Luca choked. "W-*What*?"

"How about a sandwich?" Frida held out a wrapped sub.

Tor shook his head. "I'm fine, thanks."

"Great. More for me." Luca swiped the sub from Frida.

She gawked at Tor. "Not in the mood for beer *or* food? Are you sick?"

"I told you—I'm fine." *My body aches.* Tor tightened his jaw and looked beyond Frida at the pouring rain.

Frida followed his gaze. "Okay, this is getting ridiculous." She pulled out her phone from her back pocket. She tapped the screen, and her eyes widened slightly. "Holy shit."

"What is it?" Luca asked, peering over her shoulder.

She held up her phone screen showing the weather radar. A swath of red and purple encompassed their current location. "We're surrounded by this storm for miles."

Harold finished refueling the SUV and approached them. "Which way is it moving?"

Checking the screen again, she furrowed her brow. "It… doesn't seem to be moving."

Harold looked sideways at Tor. "And I believe the answer is standing right there."

Tor blinked at his friends as all eyes focused on him. "It's not me."

Frida snorted. "Oh no? We haven't been able to get out of it since we left LA."

"And according to the radar, we appear to be right in the middle of it," Harold added.

Luca smirked at Tor. "So you *can* control the weather! Cool!"

Tor bristled. "No. I. Can't! Look. Are we gonna get going, or you guys gonna just stand there and make these accusations?"

Frida, Luca, and Harold exchanged glances.

"We'll be waiting around here for hours before this storm decides to let up," Harold said.

"You mean, until Tor decides to cheer up," Luca said.

"I'm. Fucking. Fine." Tor said through gritted teeth.

A crash of thunder echoed in the area and shook the ground.

Harold sighed. "We'll have no choice but to brave the rest of the way home."

They climbed back into the SUV and continued their trip. On their way to the main highway, Frida checked her phone again.

"Now look!" She held up the phone.

Luca took a giant bite of his sandwich. He peered over the front passenger seat as he chewed. Tor's gaze flitted to Frida's phone screen. The blotch of colors from the radar remained over their location, even as they moved.

Luca swallowed. "Is that storm… moving with us?"

Frida's gaze shot to Tor. "Are you still going to deny this?"

Tor tightened his fists. "For the last time!" he growled through clenched teeth. Strobes of blinding white light lit up the sky then struck down in an open field near the road. Thunder crackled then rumbled deeply, shaking the ground like an angry giant. The deep red and purple colors on the weather radar intensified.

"I think it's plainly obvious," Harold grumbled, white-knuckling the steering wheel as he fought to keep the vehicle steady.

"None of this started happening until Myollnir got stolen. How in Helheim are you doing that?" Frida asked Tor.

"I'm not doing it on purpose!" Tor snapped. Another rumble of thunder shook the ground.

"Damn it, Tor! Calm down before you cause an accident," Harold said.

Tor took a deep breath, trying to soothe his frazzled nerves. "I don't know how I'm causing this. If I knew how to stop it, I would."

"I've known you for a long time, and I've never seen you this pissed and moody before," Luca said. "Maybe that's what it is."

"Or it could have something to do with Myollnir?" Frida's gaze swiveled to Harold.

Harold grunted. "Perhaps. Tor tends to emanate a strong electrical field whenever he gets emotional."

Tor stiffened. "I'm not… getting… emotional!"

"This is the strongest that I've felt from him." Harold met Tor's gaze through the rearview mirror. "*You* may not notice anything unusual, Tor, but believe me, everyone else around you can feel your static charge."

"So if we get Myollnir back, then this crazy weather will stop?" Frida asked in a hopeful tone.

Tor slammed the back of his head against the headrest and sighed. He stared blankly out his rain-soaked window and at the wavering images of the passing landscape. Something cold touched his bare arm. He flinched, his head snapping to Luca's grinning face.

"Seriously, man. You need a drink." Luca held up the bottle of Warrior's Stout, already opened and ready.

Frida gasped. "Luca! Are you crazy? You want to get us arrested? Put that shit away!"

Luca shook his head. "Keep your panties on, Fri. It'll be fine as long as no one sees." He nudged Tor again. "C'mon."

Tor stared at the bottle. Frowning, he snatched it and took a reluctant swig. He froze. Somehow the drink tasted even more amazing. Maybe he really did need it after all. He chugged the rest in seconds. As he savored the last drop, he tasted a hint of something else. Something strange, yet familiar. Furrowing his brow, he smacked his lips.

"What's wrong now?" Luca asked, tilting his head.

Tor belched into his fist and examined the empty bottle. "I'm fine," he said absently. Then his mind went blank. *Am I getting buzzed?* he wondered. He *never* got buzzed.

"You sure? You look a little tired," Luca said.

Moments later, exhaustion came over Tor, as if he'd come down from a huge adrenaline rush. His eyelids grew heavy, and the world around him became dark. "I'm not…"

"Why don't you take a nap?"

Tor muttered, fighting futilely to stay awake. Finally shutting his eyes, he felt his body go limp.

* * *

"Look, the sun's finally coming out!" Luca leaned over the front console and pointed to a small break in the dark clouds.

"About time," Harold said.

"Thank the gods!" Frida said.

Luca beamed. "It was a long shot, but it actually worked."

Frida shifted her gaze. "What worked?"

"I slipped some of Tor's sleeping tablets in his drink."

"You what!" She peered at Tor, who slept soundly in the backseat, his head lolled to the side.

"Relax. He'll be fine," Luca assured her. "He'll be sleeping like a baby for the rest of the trip, and we can ride home in peace and enjoy the scenery." He gestured to the dissipating clouds and the blue sky greeting them.

Frida sighed and crossed her arms. "He just better not wake up cranky again," she muttered.

Luca nestled back in his seat and stared out the window at the beautiful mountainous landscape. The early-afternoon sun painted the trees and distant plateaus with a mix of earthy oranges, browns, and greens. The serene view was a stark contrast to the war going on between VanAesir and Jotnar Malice. Luca had to do something—fast. He glanced over at Tor. Strands of auburn hair concealed part of Tor's face, and a thin line of drool drizzled down the side of his chin.

He's gonna kill Tristan, Luca thought. *There has to be another way to fix this.* Fights always ended up messy. Perhaps diplomacy—and maybe a little creativity—was the real answer. It was time for Luca to put his quick wits to work. For the remainder of the trip, he devised his plan.

A door slammed, jostling Luca out of his thoughts. *We're home already?* He glimpsed the sign of the Nine Worlds Music Specialty Shop glowing in the night and perked up. "Oh yeah! Home sweet home!" He opened the rear passenger door and hopped out. He met Frida and Harold outside the back of the SUV, sorting through the luggage.

"Sid and the others will unload the trailer shortly," Harold said, handing Luca his duffel bag. "In the meantime, you guys get some rest. It's late. We'll pick things back up tomorrow."

"Thanks, Harold." Frida shouldered her bag and looked toward the backseat, where Tor was still snoozing. "What about him?"

Harold's gaze flicked to him. "I'll deal with Tor."

The front door of the dimly lit music shop opened, the Closed sign knocking against the glass. Sid, the shop owner and close friend of the band, came rushing out, followed by Colton, Dana, and Ryder, his employees. "You guys finally made it! Welcome back!" Sid said, approaching the three of them.

Luca waved. "Hey, man. It's good to be back. We'll catch up with you tomorrow, eh?"

Sid nodded. "Sure thing. That trip probably took a lot out of you guys. Don't worry. We'll take care of things from here."

Luca and Frida rounded the corner of the building and entered through the back door. The musty smell of the paper-strewn back office welcomed them. Luca trudged up the stairs behind Frida and entered their shared apartment on the second floor. He dropped his bags in the main room and approached the large window overlooking the street.

"You know there's no chance we'll be getting any practicing in once Tor wakes up, right?" Luca looked over his shoulder at Frida.

Groaning, Frida sank onto the couch and rested the back of her head against the cushions. "If we can't get Myollnir back, then we're screwed. We won't be ready by Saturday at this rate. I'm getting sick and tired of this shit. If we can't get it together, I'm leaving VanAesir."

Luca paled. A sensation of butterflies filled his stomach. "You can't leave! This band needs you."

She sighed. "It's not like I *want* to leave the band. You guys are like family. Besides, I would hate the idea of playing with someone else. But I feel like I have no choice if I'm ever going to have a real career. As much as it hurts, this is *my* future we're talking about here. I can't abandon my goals to stay with VanAesir if we keep having these problems. I'm at wit's end, Luca. If we end up not being able to play at Valhalla Injection because of Tor, I'm out."

"Tor's complicated. You know that. We can't just give up on him."

"Why? He's practically given up on himself. Let's just get him another guitar for now, so at least we'll be able to practice as a group."

Luca thought for a moment then exhaled through his nose. "Remember last April Fool's Day when I disguised one of the spare guitars as Myollnir and hid the real one?"

Frida's face softened, and she snickered. "Yeah, Tor was ready to beat your ass when he found out what you did."

"Hey, it was April Fool's, so it was fair game. I swear, Tor's so gullible, he's every trickster's dream. Anyway, he suspected something was up with the guitar, but I managed to convince him it was all in his head. He was trying to play the guitar during one of our jam sessions and couldn't. Every note he tried to play came out wrong, as if he was a newbie all over again, because the notes on Myollnir are laid out differently than on a regular guitar."

"Oh man, he was so confused and pissed about it. His face was priceless. But what does all that have to do with anything?"

"My point is, Tor *can't* really play any other guitar but his own. We *have* to get Myollnir back."

Frida crossed her arms, her face growing rigid again. "Easier said than done. What are you gonna do? Waltz up to the Giant's Tap and take it from them?"

Luca rubbed his chin. "Actually, yes."

She gaped. "That's suicide!"

"Well, you can always go ask them nicely. Doesn't Tristan still have a thing for you?"

"Fuck him. I'd rather kiss a dead snake."

Luca chuckled. "*Touché.* Then it's settled. I'm going. As a former member of Jotnar Malice, I'm probably the only one Tristan would talk to."

"Doubtful, since you kinda, y'know, *left* that band for VanAesir."

"I can at least try."

"And what if Tristan doesn't listen to you?"

"Then when Tor wakes up, *he's* going after them."

Frida shook her head. "I don't like this."

"Me neither, but it's the only way. And it's not like we have much time until Valhalla Injection. Do me a favor and don't say anything to Harold. And *definitely* don't say anything to Tor."

"I'm not saying shit. For everyone's sake, you better know what you're doing." She hopped up from the couch, marched to her room down the hall, and shut the door.

Luca swallowed a lump in his throat. Frida sounded serious, and she almost never went back on her word. VanAesir would be finished in a matter of days if they couldn't get Myollnir back—and get their shit straight.

Footsteps echoed from the stairwell, rousing Luca from his thoughts. Grunting, Harold and Ryder ascended the stairs, carrying the sleeping Tor by his arms and legs. They trudged through the open front door. Luca followed them to Tor's room at the end of the hall. The familiar bassline from one of their songs boomed from behind Frida's closed door as he passed. She must have been practicing without them. She was hard at work preparing for Valhalla Injection. Her discipline was one of the many things that Luca envied about her.

"For everyone's sake, you better know what you're doing." Her words echoed through his mind.

Harold and Ryder laid Tor on his bed. Harold waved Ryder off, and the young man quickly left the apartment.

"Tor needs to go on a diet," Harold said with a huff.

Luca stared at Tor, trying to find the smallest ounce of fat on him.

"Anyway," Harold continued, "we need to figure how to best handle this problem. Knowing Tor, he'll rush right up to Tristan's doorstep. No one is going anywhere near Jotnar Malice until we have a plan."

"Can't you foresee anything?"

"Luca, I just finished driving a seventeen-plus-hour trip from LA to Seattle. I'm too exhausted to concentrate on my foresight. Tomorrow, my mind will be clearer."

Luca watched him leave Tor's room and stop at Frida's door. Harold knocked, and the music stopped. Moments later, the door opened. While

Harold and Frida talked, Luca crept out of Tor's room and made his way to the front door. The next morning would be too late to figure out a plan. There was only one thing to do, and Luca knew he was the only one who stood a sliver of a chance at being successful. He slipped out the door and rushed downstairs.

CHAPTER SEVEN

Luca stared out the window of the metro bus heading downtown. The glow of the passing streetlights whisked across his face in a steady rhythm.

"Did you hear about all that crazy weather down in Cali earlier?" Luca heard a young man sitting adjacent to him say to his female friend. They were both dressed in all black, their short black hair dyed with dark-blue streaks. The man stretched his legs, his All Star sneakers peeking out from beneath his baggy skater pants.

"Freaky, man," the woman said. "Thunderstorms in LA? Maybe the zombie apocalypse is about to happen, too." They both snickered.

Luca frowned. Their voices became a light buzz as he tuned them out and continued staring out the window. The bus turned a corner, and he made out the Giant's Tap building in the distance. He chewed his bottom lip. How was he going to explain himself, returning to a place he hadn't been in nearly three years?

The bus stopped at a covered bus stop a block away from the bar. Luca got off and trudged down the street as if it were the longest walk of his life. The Giant's Tap was his old stomping grounds, where he'd first gotten his big break as a musician, becoming one of Jotnar Malice's rhythm guitarists. Subleased by the members of Jotnar Malice, the pub hosted local bands regularly. Tristan had a lot of clout for being the start of many popular bands' early careers. When Luca decided to quit Jotnar Malice to join VanAesir, it was a big choice, one he'd thought he might regret. But it'd turned out to be the best decision he'd ever made when Tor, who had quickly become one of his best friends, introduced him to the drums, his new love.

Luca stood under the bar's awning and stared in the window at the hanging lit-up sign of the band's logo—a serpent entwining a snowflake. He swallowed. *It's now or never…*

Entering the dimly lit bar, Luca concentrated on giving his face generic features that would make him look like any other young man in a bar. He wouldn't reveal his true self until he found Tristan. A whiff of familiar scents of the past overtook him as he wove through the crowded bar. Beer on tap, sweat, iron… pleasant memories of home. Death metal music boomed from the small stage, where two guys and two women dressed in black performed. A crowd of spectators had gathered around the stage, headbanging and rocking out with drinks in hand. Their faces were all unfamiliar. The fans and the staff were new since he'd last been there. No one seemed to pay him any mind as he approached the bar and slid onto an empty stool.

"What'll it be, man?" the bartender shouted over the noise.

Luca glanced at the selection on tap. There were far more than he remembered. Thankfully, his favorite brand, Frostmead, was still there. He was surprised to also see Warrior's Stout among the choices. He nodded once to the bartender, pointing to the cinnamon-flavored Frostmead.

The bartender drew his drink, and Luca slid money across the bar. He spun on his stool and nursed his Frostmead while he observed the crowd. There was no sign of Tristan or the rest of Jotnar Malice. And there was no telling where Tristan was hiding Myollnir. Unlike Tor, Luca couldn't sense its presence.

A young woman in a purple-and-black dress and fishnet stockings approached the bar to stand next to him. She sported a tattoo of Jotnar Malice's symbol on the left side of her exposed neck.

Luca recognized her. Dahlia Simons was the quiet and reserved keyboardist. They'd only played together a short while. He flashed her a smile. "Hey. Have you seen Tristan?"

A glass of an amber-colored drink slid to Dahlia, and she looked sideways. "Who's askin'?"

"Just a hardcore fan hoping to get his autograph."

"You and a million other fans." She downed her drink.

Luca chuckled as she set down her empty glass and left. *She hasn't changed a bit.* He watched her weave through the crowd toward a roped-off narrow hallway at the back of the bar. He knew what lay beyond those ropes: a posh, comfortable lounge where the band members spent most of their time practicing and hanging out. It was also the only way to access the stairwell that led up to the living space above. The lounge was a world beyond the business of music and running the bar. It was a place Luca had once called home. After gulping down the rest of his drink, he followed Dahlia. At the entrance to the hallway, he was immediately stopped by a bouncer.

"Read the sign," the tall, burly man said, thumbing at the sign over the doorway, which said Employees Only.

Luca watched hopelessly as Dahlia headed down the dark hallway and disappeared around a corner. He turned back to the bouncer. "I'll have you know that I was Jotnar Malice's elite rhythm guitarist back in the day. You should show me a little more respect."

The bouncer snorted then grabbed Luca by the front of the shirt, lifting him. "Listen, punk. I don't give two shits who you claim you were. No one gets past here." The man's knuckles whitened, and the muscles of his exposed forearms clenched.

Yeesh. Luca concentrated, shifting his illusionary disguise to Tristan's identity. "No one gets past? Not even your boss?"

The man started, releasing him. "What the—!"

The brief distraction was just enough for Luca to slip past and hop the ropes. Luca's mind was rattled as he sprinted down the hall, and he lost his concentration. He shed his illusionary disguise.

"Get back here!" The bouncer's booming voice echoed as his footsteps thundered down the hall.

Light peeked out from under a door ahead, and Luca made a beeline for it. He flung open the door, relieved that it wasn't locked. Familiar death metal music filled his ears. He dove inside, the light from the mid-sized room's neon wall signs and overhead track lighting encompassing him, and kicked the door closed with his foot. He inhaled the hint of a familiar rose-scented perfume—one that Scarlet always wore.

Everyone immediately stopped what they were doing to stare at Luca in shock.

Luca smiled nervously and waved. "Ah… hey, guys."

The door suddenly burst open behind Luca, the wind from the close-swinging door tickling the hairs on the back of his neck. He slipped behind the door and hid as the bouncer lumbered in. Peeking out, he stared at the man's back. Luca held his breath. His heart began pounding faster.

"Sorry, boss," the bouncer said to Tristan, who sat on the couch, his strong arms straining as he struggled to hold Myollnir in a playable position, "some asshole snuck past the ropes, and—"

Eric set his bass on its stand and slowly lifted his finger, pointing in Luca's direction, but Tristan slapped his hand away. "No one came through here," Tristan said.

Eric furrowed his brow at him but stayed silent. The bouncer nodded once then turned to leave. The door closed, and Luca exhaled, pushing away from the wall. Zeke and Eric rushed him and tackled him to the ground.

"Dude! I didn't come here to fight!" Luca yelped, struggling beneath the two stronger men. "Can we call a temporary truce? I need to talk to you." He looked up at Tristan, who straightened on the couch.

"A truce." Tristan scoffed.

Scarlet hopped up from the couch amid a haphazard stack of manuscript paper and knelt before Luca. She grabbed his chin with one hand, forcing him to look at her. "You have some nerve showing your pitiful face around here." She sneered, her eyes emitting a fiery glow.

Luca shuddered. *Maybe this was a stupid idea, after all...*

"Let him go." Tristan gestured to Scarlet, Eric, and Zeke. "Let's hear what he has to say."

The fire in Scarlet's eyes disappeared, and she reluctantly released Luca's face. Zeke's and Eric's grips slowly loosened from his arms. Zeke posted up by the door and crossed his arms.

Glancing at Zeke, Luca chewed his bottom lip. *No escape...* He stood, rubbed his face and bruised arms, and acknowledged Tristan.

"Why are you here, traitor?" Tristan asked.

Luca's mind raced as he felt all eyes bearing down on him. "I'm not a traitor. Back then, I saw opportunity, and I took it. But I realized it was a mistake."

"You're damned right it was a mistake!" Tristan slammed his fist on the couch's arm. "You left us for that bastard Tor!"

"Yeah, I know, and I regret it, big time. I should have never left you guys, my family."

"Family?" Dahlia interjected with a snicker. "You're calling us *family* now? You have no right. You'll never be welcomed back here, Luca, so don't even think of trying to kiss our asses."

Luca shrugged. "I guess I had that coming. Well, I'm definitely not gonna stick around VanAesir for much longer. The band is falling apart. Tor's gone even more berserk ever since his guitar got stolen. I swear, he's going to start Ragnarok with that uncontrollable rage."

Tristan smirked. "Tor knows whodunit, huh?"

"Of course he does. And when he wakes up, he's gonna come after you."

"Don't believe his bullshit, Tristan," Eric said, shaking his head. "Tor's probably curled up somewhere, crying like a baby over his lost toy. He's too distraught to do shit."

Tristan crossed his arms. "Of course he is. He thinks he's unstoppable with his special guitar. Tell me another story, Luca."

"It's not bullshit. For once, I'm being serious. That crazy storm in Cali wasn't a freak of nature. It was Tor's doing."

Tristan made a fleeting gesture. "So? Tor is throwing a little tantrum because his toy is gone. Big deal."

Luca hardened his gaze. "In all the years I've known Tor, I've never seen that happen. Not until you took Myollnir. He's connected to it more than any of us will ever know. Just give it back to him before shit hits the fan."

A brief silence passed as all eyes turned to Tristan. "I'm not in the mood to fight," he finally said. "I'll make you a deal, instead."

Luca perked up. Tristan was talking his language. "What kind of deal?"

"A nice one. If VanAesir can't go on without Myollnir, that means Frida is free. I want to ask her out at our big promo party on Friday. Bring her to me, and I'll consider returning Myollnir."

"Consider"? Luca lifted an eyebrow. Attempting to convince Frida of anything was like trying to give a feral cat a bubble bath. "What kind of a deal is that if you're not guaranteed to follow up on your end?"

"As I said, a nice one."

"Sounds like bullshit, if you ask me. How about I just let Tor wreak havoc in this place?"

Tristan shrugged. "We can always build a new bar. But Myollnir is one of a kind. I welcome him to try and pry it from my hands."

Yeah, your dead hands…

"Tristan…" Scarlet's face flushed with concern.

Tristan looked sidelong at his sister then back at Luca. "I know you're not the confrontational type. I know you'd just hate to have this end in a bloody fight. So agree to the deal."

"Yeah, and afterward, you and Tor can try out for Valhalla Injection next year—after you've found yourselves a new bassist," Zeke added with a grin.

Luca sighed. "Fine. I'll bring her to you. You just better hold up your end of the bargain and give Myollnir back."

"I knew you'd see it my way," Tristan said.

"Fifty bucks says Luca won't even get that woman to budge," Eric muttered to Tristan.

Tristan grinned at his bassist. "This'll be entertaining."

"You'll be fifty bucks broke," Luca said to Eric then focused on Tristan. "In fact, I won't even *have* to bring her here. She'll come on her own, and she'll be begging for you to ask her out."

Tristan laughed. "To see Frida beg would be quite the sight."

Scarlet crossed the room and stood before Luca. The pupils of her amber eyes flared briefly in a fiery spark. "For your sake, this better not be a trick."

He held his head up high and firm. "It's not. Frida will come to you as promised."

"I'll be waiting." Tristan retrieved a small black box from his pocket and ran his fingers over it.

Luca willed himself not to cringe. *That's not what I think it is…?*

Tristan's gaze flicked back to him. "We're done talking. Get the fuck out," he said, and then gestured toward the door with a faint nod.

Luca strode to the door, brushing past Zeke, who reluctantly stepped aside. "And here I thought I'd be welcomed back here like the good ol' days." Luca said, placing his hand on the knob.

Tristan snorted. "Those days were long gone as soon as you left."

CHAPTER EIGHT

No, not again, Tor thought, staring up at the giant faceless beings that surrounded him—trapping him like a wounded animal. *Didn't this just happen five times already? Why does this keep repeating?*

The air grew tense. His heart raced. With a mighty roar, he lashed out at his enemies with his fists, fighting tirelessly. But all his strength was no match for them. A crushing blow to the head killed him instantly. Tor opened his eyes and saw himself lying with his skull cracked open, his blood pooling beneath him and staining the snowy ground.

Tor awoke and stared into the cartoon lightning-bolt sheets covering his face. He strained to sit up in bed, but something restrained his limbs. His heart pounded furiously, his chest burning as he gasped for air, as though he'd run a marathon. In a fit of rage, he violently tossed and turned. He momentarily felt weightless, and his heart leaped into his throat.

Bang! Pain shot through the back of his head as it hit something solid. Unlike what he'd experienced before, that *felt* real. Growling, Tor finally ripped himself free from the tangle of bedding then found himself on the floor, face-to-face with his nightstand. He rubbed the throbbing painful area on the back of his head and frowned.

Sunlight peeked through the slats of his closed window blinds, casting lined patterns of orange-yellow light on his bedroom door. Tor crawled to his feet, sat on the edge of his disheveled bed, and took several slow breaths. Running his hands over his scraggly bed-hair, he felt his fast-beating heart begin to ease. *Just a dream,* he kept telling himself.

His hands shook as a familiar feeling of emptiness came over him. A part of him was gone. Missing. *Myollnir...* His disturbed mind began to slowly recount bits and pieces of yesterday's events. "Tristan..." he growled, balling his shaky hands into tight fists. *I'm going to kill that son of a bitch...*

Tor got dressed and left his room. Right away, he noticed the deathly quiet lingering in the rest of the apartment. After checking every room, he realized he was alone. Where were Luca and Frida this time of morning? There was only one last place to check.

He left the apartment and headed downstairs to the shop's back office. Approaching a door marked Storage, he heard the faint sounds of drums pounding beyond. He opened the door and descended another set of stairs leading into the basement. Bright track lighting illuminated the small area, becoming muted in the grey acoustic foam padding affixed to the walls.

Sitting behind his eight-piece drum set, Luca headbanged to the wild beat he played. Frida stood across from him, playing the familiar, deep rhythmic bassline of "War Edda." Her eyes were closed, and like Luca, she appeared lost in the music.

The song was missing its lifeblood—the thundering riffs of Myollnir. Frustrated over his missing guitar, Tor growled and ripped out the cord from Frida's small amp. The sounds of her bass went silent.

Frida stopped playing and scowled at Tor. "Excuse you!"

Luca stopped drumming, noticed Tor, and rolled his eyes. "Morning, sunshine. Ready to practice?"

Tor sneered. "With *what* guitar?"

"We got you a spare from upstairs," Frida said, gesturing to a cherry-red short-scale electric guitar sitting on a stand. "Sid said he didn't mind you borrowing it for a while."

"You guys aren't even the least bit concerned that Tristan has Myollnir?" Tor said.

"Of course, we are," Frida said. "But Harold told us to stay put until we figure out a plan. He's on his way over. Let's make good use of our time while we wait."

"There's no need for a plan. I'm going right over there and getting it back." Tor flicked his gaze at Luca. "You're with me, right, man?"

Their eyes locked. Luca flushed then quickly turned to switch out his drumsticks. "Uh, s-sorry. Not this time. It might not be a bad idea to wait and see what sort of insight Harold can give us."

"Besides, we need to practice, remember?" Frida reminded. "We have two days left. Or do you not want to win on Saturday?"

Gritting his teeth, Tor marched over to the spare guitar and slung the neck strap across himself. "This is a waste of time. Harold's got one hour, then I'm going after Tristan myself." He reset the small amp, plugged in his guitar and Frida's bass, and adjusted the controls.

Luca gave him a nervous smile. "Don't worry; he'll be here soon. Now don't go get all upset again and ruin the beautiful, sunny morning."

Tor rolled his eyes. "For the hundredth time, I don't control the weather."

"Right. Then we'll pretend that freak of nature didn't happen yesterday."

"But, I didn't—"

"After practice, boys!" Frida barked.

Luca raised his drumsticks. "Ready."

"Ready!" Frida said.

Tor scowled at them then averted his gaze. "Ready..."

"Two! Three! Four!" Luca came down fast and furious on the drums with the opening solo to "Death Knell." Tor tried to stay focused on the beat, but his worried mind continued to race. Frida came in on cue with her fantastic rhythmic bassline that gave the song its enchanted yet mysterious vibe. Tor bobbed his head and listened for his cue, but even the song didn't sound quite right. It was turning him off. The song's intro slowly rose until it reached its peak, signaling Tor's cue.

Tor attacked the first note and cringed. The twanging sounds the guitar produced completely zapped the song's dark nature. There was no feeling, just a jumble of sounds that had no meaning. He concentrated hard on the song, but his heart felt hollow without Myollnir. He stopped playing and looked at his friends.

Luca met his gaze, a hesitant look in his eyes. He and Frida halted playing, as well. "Did you forget how to play the song?" Luca asked.

Tor sneered. "No. I told you this ain't gonna work."

Frida sighed and tightened a string on her bass. "You can do this, Tor. Just… try, all right? Let's at least get through this one song."

"I *am* trying." Tor clenched his jaw. "Fine. Let's do it again, from the top."

They restarted the song, and Tor closed his eyes and concentrated again. On cue, he strummed his riffs without stopping this time. He gritted his teeth, the ear-piercing sounds of his guitar becoming unbearable. He then realized he was the only one playing. He opened his eyes. The result of his cringe-worthy performance was evident on his friends' contorted faces.

"That sounded horrible," Luca said, tossing his drumsticks down. "Tor, you're not complementing Frida at all."

Tor flared his nostrils. "It's not my fault you got me this damned spare. The frets feel completely different on this neck."

"Enough!" Frida barked. "We've a lot of work to do and only a few days to do it. For once, can we all just focus?" She glared at Tor. "Look, I know how much Myollnir means to you, but we have to practice, no matter what. Can you *try* adapting to the fret placements on this guitar? We have two days to get it right. I'm damn sure not going to lose to that asshole Tristan!"

Tor swallowed and glanced down at the guitar strings. The instrument felt too foreign to him. There was no way he could get used to these super-narrow frets in just two days. He gave the strings an idle strum, expecting to hear one chord but instead producing another eerie-sounding mess that sent a shiver down his spine.

His blood boiled. *I can't do this to Brock. I must get Myollnir back.* "Fuck!" He ripped off the neck strap and returned the guitar to its stand. "Tristan's going to pay for this!"

"Whoa!" Luca popped up from his stool. "Where do you think you're going? Harold's not here yet."

"Who cares!" Tor's vision became an electrified haze. The world around him transitioned to a bluish tint. His arms tingled as streams of electric power surged through his veins.

"Hey, Tor," Luca said. "Calm down, all right? You can't leave. Not yet. I need you to—"

"Try to stop me." Tor flexed his forearm as a warning, electric sparks traveling down to his fist.

Luca paled then slowly lowered himself back onto the stool.

Tor marched to the door. "I'll be back—*with* Myollnir." He flung open the basement door and discovered Harold standing there, his face as dark as a stormy sky. "Out of my way, Harold."

Crossing his arms, Harold lifted his head slightly, remaining posted in the doorway like a statue. "Looks like I got here just in time. Going somewhere?" His eyes gave off an amber glow.

"None of your damned business." Tor raised his hands, about to shove Harold out of the way. "Now mo—"

Before Tor's hands could reach Harold's chest, Harold grabbed one of his wrists. The electric current surged into him, and he shuddered and cringed, but didn't let go. He gave Tor's wrist a firm, skillful twist.

Tor's eyes went wide. Pain instantly shot up his arm, causing him to sever his concentration over his electric power. His blue-tinted, electric-hazed vision returned to normal. He fell to his knees, at the man's mercy. "Ow! Stop! You're gonna break my arm!"

"That would be financially devastating," Harold said in a calm voice. He let himself in, closed the door behind him, and finally released Tor. "Stay."

Wincing, Tor straightened and rubbed his sore wrist. "I'm going to get Myollnir back. Now."

"You'll do no such thing. Not without a plan." Harold's amber eyes narrowed. Then he regarded Luca. "Now what was so important that you needed to talk about?"

Tor lifted an eyebrow at Luca.

Luca smiled nervously. "Well, uh… about last night…" He tapped his fingers together.

Tor felt a sinking feeling. Was Luca, his supposed best friend, really keeping important information from him?

Luca met Tor's gaze, and he pursed his lips.

Tor stiffened. *He* does *know something. Something big.* "Luca?" Rage surged through his veins. He lunged at Luca, grabbed him by the shirt collar, and yanked him close until their noses almost touched. "What did you do? What do you know? Huh?"

"Whoa! Wait! Hear me out!" Luca pleaded, holding his hands up in surrender. "I'll explain everything! I swear!"

Harold firmly slapped his hand on Tor's shoulder. "Let him go."

Seething, Tor swiveled his gaze to his manager's glowering face. The menacing glow that returned to Harold's eyes was enough to send a small shiver down his spine. Tor reluctantly shoved Luca away.

Harold pulled his hand away from Tor's shoulder, and he turned back to Luca. "All right. Out with it."

Cringing, Luca smoothed out the wrinkles in his shirt collar and took a step back, widening the distance between him and Tor. "Well, uh… I paid a visit to the Giant's Tap last night. And, uh… sorta made a deal with Tristan…"

Tor's mouth hung open. "Deal? You made a *deal* with that bastard who stole from me? Are you fucking serious?" Electric streaks filled his vision. "I can't believe you went behind our backs and did that!"

"It's not what it looks like," Luca assured.

"I have to go with Tor on this," Frida said, scowling. "I thought you were going to go talk to Tristan, not make deals with him."

Tor snapped his head to Frida. "You knew about this? You didn't tell me?"

Frida lifted her chin. "I had no idea of the extent of his plan. Besides, you were sleeping."

Harold cleared his throat, and all eyes turned to him. "And this is why I told you three to stay put." He made a sour face as he gestured to Luca with a flick of his wrist. "Go on."

Luca took a deep breath. "Tristan does have Myollnir, as we suspected. I saw it myself. The good news is he might give it back."

Tor blinked, a shred of relief filling his chest. But something else niggled his brain, a bad feeling. "Wait. What do you mean he *might* give it back?"

"Well…" Luca chewed his bottom lip.

Here we go. Tor exhaled a puff of air.

Luca turned to Frida and cringed. "Tristan wants to ask you out, Fri."

Frida snorted a laugh. "You're joking, right?"

Luca shook his head. "Hey, all you have to do is go see him at the Giant's Tap, and he'll give back Tor's guitar."

"I am not stepping foot anywhere near that gods-forsaken place!"

Tor paused and thought about the absurdity of Tristan's request. "You mean to tell me Tristan stole *my* guitar just so he can get into Frida's pants?"

"Excuse me? *No one* is getting into my pants!"

Luca shrugged. "I guess he's desperate for a little T&A?" He gave a light chuckle.

Frida's dagger-sharp gaze speared through Luca.

"There's got to be more to this," Harold said, looking contemplative. "It's just too ridiculous otherwise." He put his finger to his temple, and his expression went blank.

Tor rubbed his chin. "I have an idea. Fri, go there, pretend to be interested, and while he's distracted, I'll sneak in and get my guitar back."

Luca slapped his forehead. "That's a terrible idea, Tor. Leave the scheming to me."

Frida's cheeks flushed a deeper shade of red. "You've got to be insane to think that I'd go anywhere near that asshole who apparently considers me some sort of commodity! I've talked to him a few times, yes, as mutual friends, and I sort of suspected he had a thing for me, but there was no way in Helheim I'd ever be interested. I've heard the horror stories about his past relationships. He's a spoiled little boy who will go to extremes to get what he wants. I'd rather drink rat poison than pretend to be interested in him!

"How fucking selfish are you, Tor, to not even care about my feelings, or for you to think I'd pretend to go along with some charade and potentially put myself in a dangerous position, all for the sake of getting your precious guitar back? Is Myollnir seriously worth more than me, your supposed friend?"

"What? No! Of course not!" Tor said in a panicked voice. "I just thought it would be easier if—"

She gritted her teeth. "You know what, fuck you. Fuck all of you. I'm not going to be a part of this." She grabbed her bass, stormed out of the basement, and slammed the door so hard, the walls rattled.

Tor and Luca jumped. Harold flinched, breaking out of his meditative state.

"That went well," Luca said.

Tor stared at the door and chewed his bottom lip. "Harold, is… is she—"

Harold shook his head. "She's not leaving the band… yet. But I advise that something gets done about this *quickly*."

"How are we going to get Myollnir back without her?" Tor asked.

Harold scratched the stubble over his jaw. "She doesn't need to go to the Giant's Tap—at least, not directly."

Luca perked. "You foresee something?"

"Yeah, I do, and Tor's not going to like it."

Tor widened his eyes. "What do you mean? Is Tristan going to destroy Myollnir?"

"No." Harold paused a beat and stepped closer to Tor. "How far are you really willing to go to get it back?"

What kind of question is that? Tor balled his hands into fists. "I'll do anything. You know that."

A hint of a smile appeared on Harold's normally stoic face. "*Anything?*"

Oh, fuck…

Chapter Nine

He's smiling. Tor stared warily at Harold's back as he and Luca followed their manager upstairs to the apartment. Whatever plan their manager had in mind couldn't be good if it made him smile. But he'd apparently gotten a glimpse into the future and whatever amusement it held. Tor took a deep breath. So long as Harold's plan would get Myollnir back, that was all that mattered.

Tor shut the front door behind him and stood before Harold in the main room, crossing his arms. "What's the plan?"

Luca sighed and plopped onto the couch with a soft bounce. "This had better be good."

"Get yourself some new clothes and borrow Frida's bolero," Harold instructed to Tor. "You're going to need it if you intend to sweep Tristan off his feet."

Tor choked on his breath. "W-Wait… *What*?" *First, he smiles. Now, he's cracking jokes?*

Luca burst out laughing. "Harold! That's hilarious! That's genius! I couldn't have thought of a better plan myself!"

"You have *got* to be kidding me," Tor said. *Harold's been hanging around Luca too long.*

"It's your best bet at getting Myollnir back," Harold said. "Trust me."

"By dressing up as Frida?"

"You *do* have a cute face." Luca grinned, patting Tor's stubbly cheek.

Tor growled and slapped his hand away. "Shut up."

"Listen," Harold explained. "I know the plan sounds… strange. But Frida is Tristan's weakness, so you need to exploit it. His guard will be dropped, and Myollnir will be yours for the taking."

Tor frowned as he considered the plan. "Tristan wouldn't really give Frida my guitar… would he?"

"He might… if you ask nicely."

Tor snorted. "Tristan's not stupid. He'll recognize me. I mean, come on. For one, I'm, like, ten shades lighter than Frida."

"Cosmetic. Easy fix," Luca countered.

"Okay, smartass. What about the fact that I'm six-four and Frida's five-eleven?"

"Frida sometimes wears those black spiky boots with the platform heels. Another three inches right there," Luca said, wagging his finger. "Close enough that I'm sure Tristan would be too lovestruck to notice a two-inch difference. Anyway, he's still taller than you."

"I am *not* wearing her shoes!"

"Don't worry. I can disguise your shoes to look like hers."

"No." Tor gritted his teeth. "I'm not doing this. I hate Tristan's guts, and you guys want me to flirt with him? As *Frida*?"

"Well, you did sort of ask Frida to do the same," Harold reminded.

Tor wrinkled his nose and turned to Luca. "Why don't *you* do this? You're better at disguises and tricks."

Luca shrugged. "I am, but it's your guitar, and you're the only one who can carry the thing."

Tor sighed. He was running out of excuses to not go along with the absurd plan. Dress as a woman? Dress as *Frida*? He adored her, but not *that* much.

"C'mon, Tor," Luca continued, playfully draping his arm around his shoulders. "It'll be fun. I'll join you. I need to be nearby to maintain the disguise, anyway. Besides, I wanna get a good look at Tristan's googly eyes when he sees you." He snickered.

"Great. Tristan will know it's a trick, for sure." Tor shrugged Luca off.

"Nope. 'Cause I'm gonna disguise myself, too. I'll be your, uh… number one VIP superfan. Yeah! I'll just say I entered a random contest and won the ultimate prize of spending a fan day with Frida."

"Ugh."

"I like it, Luca." Harold nodded. "Make it happen."

Tor whipped his head back and forth between them. *I can't believe I'm doing this…* "Shouldn't we at least tell Frida? I doubt she'd be cool with me pretending to be her."

"Let's find out!" Luca grabbed his hand and tugged him to her bedroom door.

Tor growled and yanked his hand away. "Stop. I'm not going to do this!"

Harold's eyes glowed a faint amber color, and he smirked. "I don't think Frida would mind."

Tor grimaced, hoping that for once in his life, Harold's prediction would be wrong.

Luca knocked. "Hey, Fri! It's safe to come out now. We came up with the perfect plan!"

Moments passed, and the door finally flung open. Frida glowered at Luca then Tor. "Leave me alone about Tristan."

"But you didn't hear the awesome plan," Luca said then elbowed Tor in his side.

Tor grimaced and rubbed his side. Meeting Frida's cold stare, he sighed and muttered, "Let me borrow your bolero…"

Frida's expression shifted from disbelief to horror as Tor, Luca, and Harold explained the plan. Silence fell over the room for several long moments. Tor watched her expectantly. Her silent, still reaction left him on edge. Finally, her face softened a little, then her shoulders slumped. She let out a snort and a snicker, then at last, she threw her head back and howled with laughter.

"Oh man. That is the funniest thing I've ever heard!" Frida wiped her eyes.

She's laughing? Tor had rarely managed to make her smile, much less laugh. While it was normally refreshing to see her in high spirits, right now, he was quite disturbed by it. "Y-You're not going to be mad if I impersonate you?"

"Mad? Tristan deserves every dirty trick and more for what he's done to you." She smirked. "Humiliate him good for me. His vain ass needs it."

Tor flared his nostrils. "As long as I don't have to kiss him."

"Eww! I'd sooner kiss a toilet seat before I'd ever lock lips with him." She paused and looked him up and down. "You're going to need a serious makeover. And I'm not giving you my bolero. Your broad shoulders will rip it apart."

"He needs it," Harold pointed out. "You wear it to all your gigs. It's a signature part of you, and something Tristan will expect to see."

Frida grumbled. "Okay, fine. But just… drape it around your shoulders or something. Seriously, Tor, if you rip one thread—"

"I'll take good care of it," Tor said.

She examined him again. "You'll need new clothes, new shoes, a wig… We'll head to my favorite boutique downtown. And you'll definitely need a shave." She ran her fingers down his beard stubble. "Damn. I don't think all the makeup in the world will make you look remotely feminine. Maybe if you manage to get Tristan really drunk, he won't know the difference."

"Leave the facial disguises to me," Luca said.

Tor cringed. "Hey, don't overdo it, Luca."

"Don't worry. While I'm near you, I'll be able to maintain my concentration."

"Oh! I forgot!" Frida continued. "You're also going to need to wear a corset."

Tor blinked. "A *what*? Oh, *fuck* no!"

Harold brought his fist to his lips and cleared his throat, hiding his smile.

Luca burst out laughing. "Damn, Tor, you'll be looking so sexy, you're gonna make *me* want to ask you out!"

"Shut up!" Tor growled then turned back to Frida. "I'm not wearing a damned corset."

Frida crossed her arms. "You need some kind of figure. Trust me, it will work."

"No."

"Tor." Harold's lips twitched as though he were fighting down another smile. "If there's anyone who can turn you into a convincingly attractive woman, it's Frida."

"Yeah, and remember Myollnir," Luca said in a singsong voice.

Tor clenched his jaw then let out an exasperated growl. *Is this really happening right now?* "All right, fine. Let's do this…"

* * *

Tor never realized being a woman was such hard work. He'd spent a whole day with Frida, learning seemingly simple things like mannerisms and how to walk and sit properly. Tor had struggled to keep up with her crash-course lessons. He'd stopped counting the number of times she'd face-palmed due to his clumsiness.

"How many times do I have to tell you to close your legs!"

Tor jolted out of his thoughts and stared up at Frida's scowling face. Tomorrow night was the party, and Tor didn't feel like he'd made much progress. He grunted and straightened in the uncomfortable kitchen chair, the hard wood making his ass sore. "Like this, right?"

Frida slapped her forehead. "Now you're sitting like you have a stick up your ass. Watch me again." She pulled out a chair, carefully sat, and crossed her legs.

"Sit with more class and grace, Tor!" Luca called, poking his head out from his bedroom.

Tor growled, annoyed that Luca thought the lesson was the perfect opportunity to make jokes. "No one asked the peanut gallery. Now leave us alone!"

Snickering, Luca disappeared back into his room and shut the door.

Returning to the lesson, Tor stood from the chair then sat down again, slowly, crossing his legs. He cringed. "Ow. My knee digs into my calf when I do that, and it hurts. How do you women do this all the time?"

Frida snickered. "We're resilient. Now quit complaining, you big baby."

He gave her a half-hearted smile. "Thanks for helping me, by the way."

Her face softened, and she gave him a small nod. "Hey, if it means getting back at Tristan, I'll do anything."

His legs started aching and falling asleep, so he quickly uncrossed them and sat in his usual, sprawled position. "I'm sorry about what's been happening to the band. I never wanted any of this to happen. It devastates me to know that you would even consider leaving VanAesir..."

Seeming annoyed, she glanced at his uncrossed legs then averted her gaze. "I never wanted to leave. I'm just… tired, y'know? Tired of the same old shit. I want to see VanAesir go places. We can't do that when you can't keep things in control."

"I don't know why I have such a hard time. I never had this problem before I got this guitar. I wish you can understand what goes through my mind when I play. When I just get lost in the music. I play with every ounce of my soul. I feel so… free." He tapped his fingertips together as he tried to think of the right words.

"Musical orgasm. I understand." She nodded sagely.

He flushed. "It—It's not sexual or anything…" *At least, I don't think it is…*

She laughed. "That's just what it's called. It's that point of consciousness you reach that feels like ecstasy, omniscience, or sublime understanding."

Tor thought about his dreams—nightmares—and the visions he'd seen while he played. "Yeah… something like that… But some of the things I see—and feel—I can't control…"

"That's your subconscious speaking out. Something inside you is calling. Maybe telling you to do something important. But only you can figure that out."

The giant... Maybe his subconscious was telling him to get Myollnir back, even though he'd had the visions long before it was stolen.

"What do you feel?" Frida tilted her head. "What do you see?"

Tor held his head and thought hard. "A monster... a giant... something that keeps kicking my ass over and over again. I feel helpless. Defeated."

"I think you just need to take a long, hard look at yourself and figure things out." She reached over and placed her hand over his. "And don't worry. I'm helping you get Myollnir back. I know how much it means to you and how much Brock meant to you. I'm not *that* heartless, y'know." She chuckled. "I know I'm hard on you sometimes, and yes, sometimes, you get on my nerves, but you are my friend, and nothing will change that."

Tor froze, staring at her warm chestnut hand covering his as he listened to her heartfelt words. Rarely did she have those moments, and it meant all the world to him now. Smiling, he placed his other hand over hers. "Thanks. That means a lot."

CHAPTER TEN

Exhaustion and hunger overwhelmed Tor as he trudged into the apartment Friday afternoon with an armful of shopping bags. They'd traveled to nearly every department store in the city throughout the week for something or another, creating Tor's ultimate disguise. *Who knew shopping could be so physically draining?* Tor thought. Harold had been smart to duck out early before he was dragged along for the shopping sprees.

After dumping the bags next to the couch, Tor plopped down on the soft cushions and exhaled. He shifted and put his aching feet up on the opposite armrest. He closed his eyes. Moments later, he felt his feet get pushed off the couch. His eyes sprang open, and he looked straight up at Frida's scowling face and Luca's smiling one.

"This is no time to be sleeping! We have work to do."

Tor groaned. "But the party's not until eight. We've four whole hours!"

"Yeah, and I still don't think it'll be enough time to work miracles on you."

Tor made a sour face.

"It'll probably take you at least an hour to put these on," Luca said, holding up a pair of what appeared to be women's lace thongs.

Tor rolled his eyes. "I know how to put on a pair of underwear. Though, I'm not wearing lace. And I'm for damned sure *not* wearing a thong."

Luca smirked. "Oh, these are not just *any* underwear."

"They look like underwear to me."

"Oh wow, I totally forgot about getting him a pair of those," Frida said. "Quick thinking, Luca."

"Hey, that's what I do."

Tor whipped his head back and forth between his friends. "What are they if they're not underwear?"

Frida averted her gaze and cleared her throat, attempting to hide her amusement.

Tor swore under his breath. "Is it going to hurt?"

Luca thought for a moment. "Mmm… not usually."

"*'Not usually'?*"

"If you wear them correctly, it won't hurt."

"And how would you know?"

Luca rolled his eyes. "What can I say? I enjoy the art of disguise."

Frida grabbed Tor by the ear and tugged him to the bathroom. "Come on, let's get to work."

"Ow!" Tor winced, reluctantly walking alongside her.

"Can I help?" Luca asked, happily trailing behind.

"I'm going to need all the help I can get," Frida said.

Fuck my life, Tor thought among the string of curses he muttered as Frida and Luca helped dress him. The Seattle skies were overcast all afternoon, reflecting his sour mood. The sooner he got this ridiculous ruse over with, the sooner he could get on with his life and play music again. *Brock's probably laughing in his grave right now.*

"Hold still," Frida ordered. She firmly secured the final hook of the chrome-spiked, black leather waist-cinching corset over his matching long-sleeved shirt. Tor lost his breath.

"Uf!" Tor braced himself on the bathroom counter. "What are you trying to do? Suffocate me?" *Women actually wear this shit?* It was bad enough he had to wear a bra stuffed with socks and wiggle into a pair of hip-hugging black leather pants that pressed painfully against his tucked jewels.

Frida gave him an apologetic smile. "It needs to fit tight enough to give you curves."

"Fuck curves. I need to breathe."

Frida rolled her eyes and loosened some of the laces in the back of the corset. He exhaled as some relief came to his midsection.

He looked in the mirror and cringed. "Please say we're done now."

"Nope." Frida left the bathroom a moment and returned with one of the dinette chairs. "Sit."

Furrowing his brow, he sat. Slowly and carefully.

"Work your magic while I fix her hair," she instructed Luca then began braiding Tor's long hair.

Tor bristled. "Who are you calling 'her'?"

Frida and Luca snickered.

"Relax," Luca said.

In horror, Tor watched Frida in the mirror. It took every ounce of his willpower to keep from pulling away. He couldn't remember the last time he'd willingly let anyone touch his hair. His gaze bounced to Luca, who gave Tor's hands a thorough manicure and polish.

"Now for the real fun part," Luca said once he finished. He placed one hand on Tor's shoulder. "Keep looking in the mirror."

Tor stared at his reflection but saw nothing different. He blinked once, and suddenly, he was looking at Frida's face, her tawny skin silky smooth and flawless. "Holy—!" He started, nearly jumping out of the chair.

Frida held him back down in the seat. "Sit still!" She continued braiding his hair all the way around his head like a beehive.

Tor grunted and cringed. "But... I'm you!"

"Trust me. You'll never be me on your best day."

Luca hummed a tune as he touched the tip of Tor's size-twelve motorcycle boots. Luca dragged his finger up Tor's calf, stopping just below his knee. The boot morphed into an image of a black calf-high platform boot secured with buckles and accented with spikes and chains.

Tor rubbed his eyes. "Isn't this going to make me even taller?"

"No," Luca said, disguising the other boot. "You're still wearing your own boots. Just don't look at them. It'll confuse your brain and disorient you when you walk. Man, I can't wait to see the look on Tristan's face when he sees you. I'm gonna snap a picture of him."

Tor grimaced. "Please don't."

Frida finished the braided beehive and covered it with a curly blond wig that looked virtually identical to her own hair texture. She styled it to match her own then examined him from the mirror. "There. Now you look remotely decent."

Tor stared at himself in the mirror. *Wow…* Who knew he could pull off looking like a woman? "Do I… look like you?"

"As close as you're gonna get," Frida replied.

"What're you talking about, Fri? We did a damned good job," Luca said. "You two could almost be twins. Tristan will be fooled for sure. Just remember, if you have to take a piss, make sure you sit." He snickered.

Frida laughed. Tor gave him the stink eye and held up his middle finger.

"All that's left are the finishing touches." Frida opened the bottom cabinet and retrieved her giant makeup bag.

"Maybe this *will* work," Tor mumbled as she started applying eyeshadow. "By the way, I'm sorry."

"For what?"

"For ever thinking that you women have it easy. Holy fucking shit. How do you guys wear all these uncomfortable things every single day?"

She snorted. "We don't."

Luca draped Frida's bolero around Tor's shoulders. "Tristan is totally gonna lose his shit when he sees you."

Tor scowled. "So long as he returns Myollnir. And I'm dead serious—he better not try and kiss me."

"You are quite kissable." Luca smirked and wiggled his eyebrows.

Tor elbowed him in the ribs.

"Ow! Careful. You may look like Frida, but you still have Tor's strength."

"Good. All the better to punch Tristan with if he gets too close for comfort."

"I'd punch him, too," Frida said, applying mascara.

Luca grunted and hobbled out of the bathroom, holding his ribs.

Frida finished applying the last of the makeup then gave him a final once-over and nodded. "One more thing." She unhooked her amber gemstone necklace and secured it around Tor's neck.

Tor sucked in a breath. "Wait… Are you sure?"

Her face was devoid of emotion. "You getting Myollnir back is more important."

"But this is your favorite necklace!"

"Exactly. And if this doesn't convince Tristan, then nothing will."

He chewed his bottom lip and gently clutched the amber jewels that hung from the golden necklace, which still carried Frida's warmth and her scent. "I will protect this with my life."

"You better. That cost me a fortune." Frida smiled slightly.

Tor stood and turned to view himself in the full-length mirror. Luca's applied facial disguise was virtually perfect, and Frida had selected an outfit that was very much her style.

"All right, Tor." Luca returned to the bathroom, now as an attractive brunette woman dressed in skinny jeans, a black T-shirt, and a matching baseball hat branded with VanAesir's logo. "Here's the deal: let me do all the talking."

Tor gawked at him. *How the fuck does he manage to look that good as a woman?* He shook his head. "Wait. What?"

"Disguising your exterior is easy. Your voice? Not so much."

Tor cleared his throat. "I can sound like a woman," he said, attempting a high-pitched, cracking voice that sounded more like an adolescent boy than Frida.

Frida cringed. "Not a chance."

Luca rolled his eyes. "Look, I'm doing the talking because I'm obviously better at it," he said in a convincingly accurate female voice.

Tor flinched. "Whoa! How'd you do that?"

"Lots of time, patience, practice, and hanging around a lot of beautiful women, like our lovely Frida." Luca smirked.

Frida gave Tor a look. "He has a point." She put her hands on her hips and regarded Luca sternly. "All right, this is a clever plan we got going here. Don't screw things up with your big mouth."

"I won't. Promise."

"In Luca language, that means you will."

"No, seriously. The future of our band depends on it. Trust me, I'll know just what to say. Leave it all to me."

Tor hung his head and heaved a huge sigh, knowing whatever Luca had planned would probably not bode well for Tor.

Chapter Eleven

So, how long will these disguises last?" Tor asked Luca as they waited outside the Nine Worlds Music Shop for a taxi.

"As long as I can maintain focus, so don't go and do something crazy and stress me out, like randomly losing your temper and clocking Tristan," Luca replied, checking his makeup in a compact mirror.

Tor cringed. If he didn't know it was Luca, he would have been easily charmed by his disturbingly convincing disguise. "You sure you weren't female in a previous life?"

Luca eyed him sideways, smirking. "I'm just very good at what I do, and I take my disguises seriously. Why do it half-assed?"

A yellow cab pulled up to the curb. A young man in a backward baseball cap waved and grinned at them. "Where to, ladies?"

Tor opened his mouth to reply, and then Luca slapped his forearm and said to the driver in his female voice, "Giant's Tap. And step on it."

Tor pried Luca's hand from his mouth and gingerly climbed into the backseat.

"What're you trying to do? Blow your cover before you even get there?" Luca whispered to Tor once they were on their way.

"Sorry," Tor whispered back then stared out the window at the passing streetlights. He glanced toward the rearview mirror and caught the cab driver's brief curious stare. At Tor's piercing glare, the driver quickly returned his eyes to the road.

Luca cleared his throat.

Tor looked at him and furrowed his brow.

Luca pointed to Tor's legs, which were spread open as he sat in his usual comfortable sprawl.

Oh, right... Tor sighed and drew his knees together.

Luca pointed to Tor's legs and crossed his own.

"No. It hurts to cross my legs," Tor said slightly above a whisper.

The driver's gaze jumped back to Tor, this time with slight surprise.

Tor gritted his teeth. "What are *you* lookin' at?" he growled in his masculine voice.

The driver started and quickly averted his gaze. "Uh, n-nothing, sir—miss—ma'am… sorry!"

Luca sighed.

Minutes later, the taxi pulled up behind a white delivery truck parked in front of the entrance to the Giant's Tap. Luca paid the fare, and as Tor climbed out of the taxi, he noticed the logo displayed on the back of the truck.

"Oh man," he muttered. "Are my eyes deceiving me, or is the most amazing restaurant in all of Seattle here right now?"

Luca got out and followed Tor's gaze. "Whoa. Taste of Vanaheim is here?"

"They must be catering Tristan's party." Tor salivated as he fantasized biting into the restaurant's famous beefsteak dish, which he always ordered. He and his friends were such frequent customers that the restaurant staff knew them by name.

"I gotta hand it to Tristan," Luca said. "He may be an asshole, but he's got good taste in food."

Tor's stomach growled. He'd been so constantly stressed over Myollnir that he hadn't eaten in over a day.

"Okay. Okay," Luca continued. "Enough about food. We have to focus."

"I know…" Tor could practically taste a juicy piece of beefsteak on his tongue. He envisioned forking a savory grilled morsel into his mouth when he suddenly lurched forward and felt a stinging pain in the back of his head.

"Hey! Get it together!" Luca's perfectly manicured hand was poised, ready to smack him again. "We have to get Myollnir."

Tor followed Luca to the front door.

Luca rested his hand on the handle and looked over his shoulder. "Remember, I do the talking. You just… stay quiet and remember everything Frida taught you. Act dashing, sexy. Ready to knock some drooling guy off his feet with your mere presence."

"I'd rather knock him out with my fist," Tor muttered.

"Right." Luca opened the door.

Tor sucked in his breath as he stepped inside the dark, crowded bar. A local band was performing on stage, the lead singer growling out guttural lyrics as sweat poured down his bearded face and long, scraggly hair. The crowd surrounding the stage hollered and headbanged to the intense beat, waving their drinks in the air. Colorful stage lightning swirled throughout the bar, flickering and transitioning to various patterns. In one corner, another group of people were gathered, helping themselves to trays of meat, vegetables, and desserts.

Tor inhaled the delectable scents as he followed Luca through the sea of grungy, black-clad spectators. Tor kept his eyes ahead, locking his sights on Luca.

A man drunkenly dancing backward suddenly stopped in Tor's path and collided with Tor's solid body, which nearly knocked the man down. The man's dark-brown drink sloshed over the edge of his mug, drops splashing onto Tor's hand.

Fuming, Tor confronted the stranger, staring eye to eye.

The man's eyes widened, and he gaped. "F-Frida? Frida Winters?" A broad smile edged his lips. "Holy shit! It's Frida Winters from VanAesir!"

Tor flinched and released him. Some people nearby turned their heads.

Damn. Tor looked around frantically for Luca, whom he'd lost in the crowd.

"Since when did you start coming to this bar?" another man asked, approaching. He rolled up his shirt sleeve, exposing his muscular arm, and pulled out a black marker from his pants pocket. "Can you sign one of my guns?"

Tor cringed. *Damn it, Luca, where are you?*

"Hey, are Tor and Luca here, too?" a woman in the crowd asked.

"Excuse me. Step aside. Comin' through." Luca said as he pushed his way through the crowd and emerged. He grabbed Tor's hand. "Sorry, Frida can't talk now. She's in a hurry." Luca started dragging Tor away.

"Who are you?" a man from the crowd asked.

"I'm Lizzie, Frida's liaison—that's who I am. Now let us through!"

Tor let Luca guide him along to the back of the bar, where a large, ominous bouncer stood guard. The hulking man stepped in front of a hallway and glowered at them. He then looked beyond them toward the trailing crowd.

Tor glanced over his shoulder. *Are they fans of both VanAesir and Jotnar Malice? Talk about conflict of interest.*

"Hey, Frida! Is it true VanAesir is playing at Valhalla Injection tomorrow?" somebody at the back of the crowd called.

"When are VanAesir and Jotnar Malice gonna do a collab album?" another unseen person asked.

Tor shuddered at the thought. *When Muspelheim freezes over…*

"Is Tor single?"

"Tell Luca I think he's hot!"

"Where did you buy those awesome boots, Frida?"

Luca held up his hand. "No more questions, please. Frida's had a long day. If you want to show your support, come see her and the rest of VanAesir at their next concert." He pointed at someone in the crowd. "By the way, I will *definitely* let Luca know you think he's hot!"

Tor listened, but didn't react to his fans' insistent questions, as much as he wanted to. He suddenly felt the hairs on his arms and the back of his neck stand on end, and a feeling of great relief swept through him. The gaping hole in his heart was slowly being filled. It had to be Myollnir. The essence of his guitar called to him. Tor yearned to hold it again and bond with it emotionally through his music once more. He peered over the bouncer's broad shoulder and into the dimly lit hallway beyond. *My guitar is somewhere through there.* But wherever Myollnir was, Tristan would not be far away.

The bouncer studied Tor. "I got the message from Tristan about you"—he glared at Luca—"but not you."

Luca tilted his chin. "The name's Lizzie. I'm Frida's liaison, as well as her hardcore-number-one-VIP superfan. She overdid it during rehearsals yesterday and lost her voice, so I'm translating."

The bouncer arched an eyebrow. "She lost her voice?"

Luca nodded solemnly then gave Tor a sideways glance.

Noticing the subtle cue, Tor rubbed his throat and whispered in a high, raspy voice, "I… can't… talk."

Grimacing, the bouncer pulled out a cell phone from his pocket and punched in a number. "She's here, boss," he said after a pause. "Yes, sir, but there's a problem… Yes, sir…" He ended the call and cast Tor and Luca a cold stare. "Wait here." He pointed to the spectating crowd behind them. "As for the rest of you, move the hell away from here *now!*"

Muttering and grumbling, the crowd dispersed, slowly returning to the corner buffet, the bar, and the stage, where the next band was setting up.

A man and woman appeared at the other end of the hallway. As they drew closer, Tor recognized the red-haired woman as Scarlet and the skinny, preppy guy wearing earplugs as Eric. The bouncer stepped aside, letting them through.

Scarlet scanned Luca up and down then acknowledged Tor with narrowed eyes. "Frida? You actually came? Is this another one of Luca's tricks?"

Tor swallowed and quickly shook his head.

Luca bounced on his heels, clapping his hands together, a wide grin plastered across his face. "Ohmygosh! Ohmygosh!" he gushed in his giddy fangirl voice. "My friend Chelsea is going to be so jealous that I met Scarlet Westgard and Eric Jacobsen in the flesh! She's, like, a *huge* Jotnar Malice fan. She listens to all your albums at least twice a day, stalks you guys online, and goes to *all* your concerts. Oh! And her brother has a total crush on you, Scarlet."

Scarlet exchanged glances with Eric and smirked. "Oh, I like her. I like her a lot."

Tor tried his hardest to maintain a straight face. *How the fuck does he do that?*

She nodded to Luca. "What's your name?"

"I'm Lizzie. It's such an honor to meet you both!" He paused and chewed his bottom lip. "I like listening to Jotnar Malice, too, but, um… I'm a huge fan of Frida. She's my hero! I started taking bass lessons 'cause of her!"

Scarlet made a face at Tor. "Ugh. Forget what I said before."

"Oh, please don't be mad, Scarlet. I like Jotnar Malice as a band better than VanAesir. I just like Frida. I don't care much for Tor and Luca. They tend to attract all the dumb, clueless fangirls. You guys are way more sophisticated than them."

Eric raised his eyebrows and thumbed toward Luca. "You sure you still wanna forget that?" he said to Scarlet.

Scarlet chuckled at Luca. "Flattery will get you everywhere, Lizzie." Her gaze bounced to Tor. "Are you really here, Frida? Is this really you? I mean, you can't possibly be in love with my brother, right? He's got so many imprints of your hand on his face— which I find hilarious."

Tor felt his heart beat faster. Sweat beaded on his palms. Was she already onto him? He took a breath and shook his head.

"What are you? A mute now?"

"Actually, yes, and that's why I'm here," Luca broke in. "She lost her voice practicing yesterday, so she wanted me to be her liaison for now."

"Lost her voice?" Scarlet's eyebrow rose.

Tor nodded quickly and rubbed his throat, feigning a look of pain.

"Yep," Luca replied. "Frida still doesn't know why Tristan wanted her to come, but she was tired of dealing with Tor and Luca, so she figured she'd come and enjoy the party."

Eric stepped forward. "Did Luca tell her about Tristan? Is he here now?" He eyed Tor and Luca carefully.

"Nah. Luca's home taking care of Tor. Apparently, Tor got sick or something. That big lug hasn't been able to leave his bed for a week, except at night when he stalks the hallways moaning about a couple of ravens chasing him."

"Got sick, huh?" Eric's gaze bounced to Scarlet. "Wow, that sucks. And so close to Valhalla Injection, too."

"What a shame." Scarlet tsked with such exaggerated disappointment that even Tor could hear the bullshit in her voice.

"Yeah, doesn't look like VanAesir will be able to perform tomorrow," Luca said with a light shrug.

"I'm sure Tristan will be in pieces over it," Scarlet said. She paused and narrowed her eyes. "Something still doesn't seem right here. Something seems… off."

"What do you mean?" Luca asked.

"I mean, these little shortcomings with VanAesir sound a little too convenient and downright suspicious. One can never be too careful, especially when dealing with people like Luca." She looked at Tor carefully. "If you're really Frida, then turn your bolero into a rope."

Tor swallowed. *What!* He chewed his bottom lip and ran his fingers through the bolero's black feathers.

Scarlet crossed her arms and cocked a hip. "Well?"

Eric cracked his knuckles in anticipation.

Tor inhaled again, watching Luca in his peripheral vision. Was it better to just give up now?

No. I can't give up. Frida didn't give up on me. I have to find a way…

Luca placed his hand on Tor's shoulder. "Hey, don't rush her, all right?" Luca said to Scarlet and Eric. "She wasn't expecting to have to show her ID…" He looked at Tor, his hand casually patting his shoulder. "Do your thing, Frida."

Tor wasn't sure if Luca was hinting something or what. At this point, he had to go for it. He carefully took off the bolero, and as he held it before them, the image of the small jacket became a lengthily coiled rope. Tor held back a gasp. *How did I do that?*

Scarlet and Eric blinked in surprise. "W-Wow… Okay, so it really *is* you," Scarlet said, then she grinned at Eric. "I don't know how Luca managed to get Frida to come here on her own, but it looks like you owe him fifty bucks."

"Damn it, don't remind me!" Eric turned and headed back down the hall.

Scarlet gestured to Luca and Tor. "All right. Follow me."

They walked past the bouncer and followed Scarlet and Eric down the hallway. As they walked, Tor noticed the image of the bolero in his hands return to its feathered form. He blinked. *An illusion?* He looked sideways at Luca.

"You're welcome," Luca mouthed.

Chapter Twelve

Eternally grateful for Luca's quick thinking, Tor felt a soothing sensation in his chest as they trekked the long corridor toward a door that opened to an illuminated private lounge. The smell of more food overpowered Tor's senses, and his stomach growled. Hoping no one heard it, Tor glanced at Eric and caught the classy pervert checking out his ass. *He's looking at Frida's ass, not mine,* Tor kept convincing himself. *He doesn't know it's me. But... it really* is *my ass in these leather pants...*

He stepped through the doorway, and the tingling sensation on his skin intensified. His heart raced as an invigorating rush of adrenaline filled his mind, instantly dissolving the stress and sadness that had recently overwhelmed him. *Myollnir's here.* Tor scanned the lounge, looking for Myollnir. Three long tables were set up along one side of the room, filled with more of Taste of Vanaheim's catered trays, and kegerators sat next to them. He scrutinized a group of instruments across the room, but didn't see Myollnir's case.

Tristan, sprawled out on the big leather couch, enjoying a frothy mug of dark-amber beer, suddenly looked toward the door. "F-Frida!" He slammed down his mug and sprang up, startling Dahlia, who was sitting in a beanbag chair across from him. Zeke, serving himself a plate of juicy tenderloins from the smorgasbord, looked over his shoulder.

Electric rage surged deep within Tor as Tristan rushed toward him with a wide grin. Tor used every ounce of willpower to restrain himself from breaking his disguise to wipe that stupid smile off Tristan's face.

Luca met Tristan halfway, blocking his path to Tor. "Aaahh! It's Tristan Westgard! It's *the* Tristan Westgard! Ohmygosh, I just wanna say you're such an amazing guitarist, and—"

Tristan halted and sneered. Zeke abandoned his food and closed in on the group, eyeing Luca suspiciously.

"Who are you? How'd you get past security?" Tristan demanded.

Eric removed the earplugs from his ears. "It's all good, man. This is Lizzie. She's Frida's liaison."

"Her what?" Tristan's scrutinizing gaze bounced from Luca to Tor as Scarlet and Eric explained the situation. "Are you serious?" he finally said, frowning.

Tor nodded solemnly and slumped his shoulders.

Tristan pursed his lips then narrowed his eyes. "No, I refuse to believe this. Of all days, she has to lose her voice today when she finally comes to see me?"

Tor shrugged and shook his head.

His face darkened. "This is probably Luca's doing. He sabotaged this somehow. His way of getting back at me for that deal we made. Did he do this to Frida?" He paused, and his eyes swiveled back and forth between Luca and Tor. "Fuck. Maybe one of *you* is really Luca."

Tor paled. *He knows?* He looked sidelong at Luca. A bead of sweat formed at the trickster's brow. *Keep concentrating, Luca.*

Luca crossed his arms. "I don't know what you're talking about. There's no trick. Luca's home taking care of Tor, who's sick."

"Trust me, brother," Scarlet broke in. "Believe it or not, this really is Frida. She proved it in a way only she can. Eric and I both saw it."

"And she can do it again!" Luca said, patting Tor on the shoulder.

Tor took off the bolero and held it up to Tristan. Its material became a coiled black rope.

"There, you see? Only Frida can do that, so are you done interrogating her now?" Luca said, casually sliding his hand off Tor's shoulder. Moments later, the image of the bolero assumed its feathered form.

Tristan's face softened. "I just needed to make sure. One can't be too careful when it comes to that trickster." Tristan paused and eyed Luca. "But what about you?"

Luca widened his eyes. "What *about* me? What the hell are you trying to say? Do I look like a guy to you?" He cupped his sock-stuffed chest for emphasis. "Sorry to say that I don't have any special powers to prove that I'm Frida's number-one superfan."

Tristan rubbed his chin. "Maybe not, but if you're really her fan, then you would know something about her that not even Tor or Luca does."

"But you do?" Luca furrowed his brow.

Oh, for fuck's sake... Tor tightened his jaw. How many more "tests" was Tristan going to give?

Tristan leaned forward, smiling at Luca. "Believe me when I say this, Lizzie—I am Frida's *true* number-one fan."

"Okay, hotshot." Luca rubbed his hands together, smirking. "I love trivia. Ask me anything."

Tor forced a smile. Did Luca really know Frida inside and out? *Gods, I hope you know what you're doing.*

"What is the name of the shade of lipstick that Frida wears only during Friday gigs?" Tristan asked.

Luca exhaled, and his smile broadened. "Vanadis Select, shade number nine—aka Bronze Shimmer— with a semi-lustrous finish. She likes wearing that shade during Friday gigs not only for good luck, but it complements the gold-colored accent on her bass." Luca turned his nose up at Tristan and snapped his fingers. "Too easy. Now, are we done with the questions?"

A hush fell over the room. Tristan looked at Luca in awe. Tor nodded in agreement and tried to keep his cool, but he was thoroughly impressed that Luca knew so many details about Frida. It was then he remembered something Luca said before. Something about hanging around Frida a lot. And taking his disguises seriously. It must've taken Luca a while to be able to study her so intricately.

"Damn. I stand corrected." Tristan rubbed the back of his head. "All right, you've convinced me enough. It just sucks that she lost her voice."

"That shouldn't matter, right?" Luca said. "You can still enjoy her company."

"That's true." Tristan beamed at Tor. "And maybe talk alone after the party."

Tor forced a weak smile. *Alone? Where?* He imagined himself alone with Tristan in his bedroom, happily smashing his head against the wall, the door, the dresser, the television…

"Whatever, I'm hungry," Scarlet said, snapping Tor out of his destructive thoughts. She wandered over to the buffet.

Eric looked toward Tristan and Tor a moment and sneered. "Looks like practice is on hold due to present company. I'm gonna go mingle for a while." He stuck some earplugs in his ears and headed for the door.

Zeke followed. "Wait up."

Dahlia nestled into a beanbag chair and stuck her earbuds into her ears. Bobbing her head, she began texting on her phone.

Tristan led Tor and Luca to the couch. Tor sat carefully, forcibly crossing his legs and resting his hands on his lap. But his fingers wouldn't stop moving, grasping handfuls of the leather fabric of his pants. *So close to Myollnir. So close to Tristan…*

"So you can't speak at all?" Tristan furrowed his brow at Tor curiously.

Tor pursed his lips. Tristan's face was very close to his; Tor could practically bite his nose off. Still, he kept his cool and responded in a high, raspy whisper. "No."

"Ugh! You sound like shit."

You look *like shit.*

"And you came willingly?"

Tor nodded.

"Frida said she's ready to quit the band after what happened at the Death by Metal concert," Luca told Tristan.

"You were great out there, as always, Frida," Tristan said. "Tor was the one who screwed things up. He always screws up your opportunities."

Fuck you. Tor plastered on a fake smile and shrugged.

"So is it true that you stole Myollnir?" Luca asked, regarding Tristan, wide-eyed.

Tristan smirked. "I borrowed it for a while."

"A long while," Scarlet muttered, chomping on a forkful of meat.

Pain shot through Tor's calf, and he uncrossed his legs, still keeping his knees together. He glanced around the room for his guitar, but it was out of sight. He felt its power calling out to him from somewhere in the direction of the stage among the other stored instruments.

"That's pretty bold. Wasn't Tor mad?" Luca asked.

Tristan shrugged. "I'm sure he was. But I wanted to prove how much of a phony he is without his precious toy. The real star of VanAesir is Frida." He smiled at Tor. "You should be front and center on stage, doing what you do best. I'm glad you finally took matters into your own hands and decided to leave."

Tor nodded curtly.

"I have something for you," Tristan continued, pulling out a small velvet box.

Tor widened his eyes. *Is that... a ring box?* Panicked, he looked over at Luca, who appeared equally surprised.

"Wait!" Luca called. "Frida's a bit overwhelmed. Let's not, uh… rush things. How about you wait till midnight to give her that? It's a full moon tonight, y'know. It'll make things extra romantic and special."

"Or maybe she'll turn into a troll." Dahlia snorted out a laugh.

"Actually, midnight sounds perfect," Tristan finally said, re-pocketing the box. He regarded Tor again, his expression softening. "All right, then." He gestured to the buffet. "In the meantime, help yourself, sweetie. There's beer and mead, too. I made sure to include your favorite, Gold Meridian."

Gold Meridian? Blech! Tor tried not to shudder as he thought about the sickeningly sweet taste of the mildly fruity mead that Frida loved.

Luca hopped up from the couch. "Wow, you're awesome, Tristan! Thanks!" He grabbed Tor's hand and dragged him to the spread.

Tor felt Tristan's eyes on him as they approached the buffet. His need to find Myollnir contended with his hunger pangs. But sensing that his guitar was somewhere in this room gave Tor some assurance. He wasn't leaving that room without it. Meanwhile, he piled his plate full with everything offered then added three extra helpings of beefsteak to another plate. At the end of the long table sat a large kegerator. Among the four offered taps was the drinking-horn-shaped tap handle of Warrior's Stout. *Tristan's got good taste in food* and *beer. I'll give him that.*

Tor reached for the Warrior's Stout handle, but Luca brushed his hand away and gave him a stern look. Tor made a face. *Does he expect me to pretend to enjoy Frida's favorite drink?*

"Nice choices," Luca said aloud. "I'm a bit of a drink connoisseur. I attend Seattle Beerfest every year.

"Try 'em all," Tristan offered. "There's plenty for everyone."

"Don't mind if I do!" Luca gave Tor a subtle wink as he began filling four mugs. The Gold Meridian was slightly lighter than the Warrior's Stout and could be easily confused at first glance. Tor kept his eyes on the correct glass as Luca casually moved them about then slid the Warrior's Stout to him.

"So, tell me." Tristan patted the seat next to him on the couch. "What are your plans now that you've pretty much ditched VanAesir?"

Tor shuddered internally at Tristan's invitation. But he swallowed his pride and went along with Tristan's bait. Skillfully balancing the plates and beer, he slowly lowered himself on the couch.

"She wants to possibly go solo," Luca replied. "She's not ready to join another band yet, if ever."

Tor nodded to Tristan, pointing to Luca.

"Fair enough," Tristan said as Tor began eating his food with awkward daintiness. "Well, I have connections to some of the local venues, so if you're ever looking for gigs, let me know. Anyone around here would love to have you. You only deserve the best. I will give you anything and everything you want. Just ask, and I'll make it happen."

Tor stopped in midchew and looked at Tristan. *Anything, eh?* He felt Luca touch his shoulder. He glanced up at Luca, who stood behind the couch. "That's really generous, and romantic," Luca said. "If only there were more guys out there like you."

"Ugh, please. Speak for yourself. One Tristan is enough," Scarlet said.

Tristan scowled at his sister. "Why don't you go hang out in the bar for a while? Take Dahlia with you."

Scarlet's eyebrows rose. "Oh? Is this where you need your 'alone' time with her?" She snorted. "Fine. But don't come crying to me when Frida adds another handprint to your face." She walked past the beanbag chair and gathered Dahlia. As the two women walked to the door, Scarlet looked over her shoulder at Tor. "By the way, Frida, you have my fullest permission to slap him as you see fit."

Tor grinned darkly. He gave her an "okay" sign and watched the two women leave.

The door slammed behind them, and Tristan glowered at the closed door. "Tch. I've never seen a more jealous woman."

Tor glanced at Luca, who gave a slight nod toward Tor's plate of food, encouraging him to continue eating. Tor was getting restless with this constant delay of obtaining Myollnir. At this point, he had no choice but to trust that Luca knew what he was doing.

"I wish I could meet a guy like you, Tristan," Luca said. "A sexy guitarist in one of the hottest bands around? Skip the dates, I'd marry you in a heartbeat!"

Tristan's smile broadened. "I'm flattered, but there's only one woman that's ever caught my eye, and I'm looking at her now."

Just... let... Luca handle it... Tor felt Tristan's gaze and half-listened to him while he enjoyed his delectable beef tips. He did his best to mind his manners and eat as carefully and properly as Frida had taught him, but before he knew it, he ended up eating everything on his plate and washing it all down with Warrior's Stout. His full belly pressed painfully against the cinched corset he'd nearly forgotten he was wearing.

"I won't lie," Tristan continued. "I've often thought about us being one of those perfect tabloid celebrity couples."

Tor emptied his mug and set it down next to the stack of plates.

Tristan gawked at the empty dishes. "Damn, woman! Hungry much?"

Luca cleared his throat.

Tor paused, realizing he might've overdone things a bit. Then again, he'd seen Frida eat and drink before. He wondered how she maintained such an amazing figure with her giant-sized appetite.

"You have no idea," Luca replied. "Since yesterday, when Luca told her the news, Frida has been so anxious to see you that she hadn't eaten since."

Tor belched in agreement.

Tristan's gaze bounced from Luca to Tor. "S-Seriously? You were that anxious to see me? Am I dreaming?"

"Trust me, it's as real as it gets. I'm so jealous she attracts the hottest member of Jotnar Malice. I'd kill to switch places with her right now." Luca sighed dreamily.

Tor blinked. *Luca... what are you doing?*

"Wow, Frida... I just want to kiss you right now." Tristan scooted closer and stroked Tor's cheek.

Tor shuddered. *The bastard wants to do* what? He glowered at Tristan's face, which slowly hovered closer to his. Tor's vision wavered to a slight bluish electric haze. He balled his hand into a tight fist, ready to imprint his knuckles onto Tristan's face.

Tristan paused midway and furrowed his brow. "Whoa... your eyes... what's with that look?"

Try kissing me again and find out.

"Ah!" Luca placed his hand over Tor's shoulder, and Tor slowly calmed his shaky fist. "Between dealing with her lost voice and her eagerness to see you, she hasn't gotten much sleep, so sometimes she has these episodes where she gets a little moody."

"She's cute when she's moody. Damn." His face lit up. "There's something else I want to show you."

Something else? While Tor exhaled in relief as Tristan left his personal space, he wondered what else Tristan had in store. Tristan hopped up from the couch and went to the group of instruments and equipment. Tristan's muscles bulged and strained as he hefted Myollnir's case and struggled to return to the couch.

Tor widened his eyes slightly. *I've seen it, and I still can't believe it. I thought I was the only one who can lift Myollnir?* He sucked in a breath then felt his hand being squeezed. He glanced sideways at Luca, noting a subtle shake of his head.

"Not yet," Luca mouthed.

"I've been waiting for this moment." Tristan clicked open the case, and with a grunt, he slowly and shakily lifted out the sparkling-grey warlock-shaped electric guitar.

Tor swallowed a lump in his throat. *How is this possible? Why is he able to pick this up? Have I lost control of Myollnir, too?*

"Ooh, are you going to play a song for Frida? This will be exciting!" Luca clapped his hands together. "This is truly the happiest day of my life! I get to hear the amazing Tristan Westgard serenade Frida with Myollnir!"

Tristan plugged a cable into an amp and adjusted Myollnir's neck strap. "You know the difference between me and Tor?"

Tor raised his eyebrows. *I'm way more handsome? More intelligent? More* talented? He faked a smile and shook his head slowly.

"Well, you *are* way hotter than Tor," Luca said, batting his eyelashes.

Tristan's face softened at Luca's comment. "Yeah, I know. I get that a lot from beautiful women like you. I'm one lucky man to have Frida finally choose me over that red-haired punk. I'm getting better at playing Myollnir, too. Won't be long until I master it. And I'll be playing it at all our shows. Unlike Tor, I'll get through all our songs, no problem. Jotnar Malice will be the number one band on the West Coast."

Tor's breath hitched. *He knows how to play Myollnir?* He rubbed his sweaty hands on his thighs. *How can that be?*

"Sounds exciting!" Luca chirped. "You guys are going to totally rock the music scene. So what are you gonna play?"

Tristan thought for a moment. "How about the opening to one of our songs? "Icingdeath"? We'll be playing it at tomorrow's event, too. Sit back and listen to real talent."

"Ooh! I love that one!"

Tor kept his eyes locked on Myollnir, biding his time.

Tristan closed his eyes and strummed a chord. Tor cringed at the grating, painful sound. It was similar to the sounds he'd made on the spare guitar. Every note was ear-piercing, terrible, and off-key. It sounded like the wailing of a dying cat. *Tristan thinks this is actually good?* Tor cast a brief look at Luca, who grimaced and rubbed his ear. *So it's not just me.*

Tristan played the final note and let the awkward sound echo throughout the room. He opened his eyes. "How's that?"

Tor wrinkled his nose and gave Tristan a thumbs-down, shaking his head.

Tristan frowned. "What? You don't like it?"

"Ah," Luca broke in. "What she meant was—"

"Frida was always a hard one to please," Tristan broke in. "She's always a challenge, constantly making you work harder. That's why I love you so much."

Luca opened his mouth to speak then quickly closed it again. He raised his eyebrows at Tor.

Tor had had enough of Tristan defiling Myollnir. It was time to make the move. He held his hands out to Tristan.

"What is it?" Tristan asked curiously.

Tor pointed to the guitar.

"She's wondering if you would let her try and play Myollnir," Luca said.

Tristan arched an eyebrow. "Now why would you want to do that? You're a bassist."

"Yeah, well, you know. She's always wanted to hold that famous guitar in her hands just once, but Tor was always so anal about never letting her touch it. Besides, you'd said you'd give her anything and everything she wanted, right?"

"Well… yeah. Is that all you want? I mean, of course, you can hold it. Well, you can try. It's very heavy, even for me."

Tor waved his hand dismissively then mockingly flexed his bicep.

"You should know that Frida is never one to give up," Luca said.

"Yeah, that's what also makes her amazing. All right, then. Just a little touch. Anything for you, dear." He unhooked the neck strap then slowly and carefully handed the guitar to Tor.

Tor exhaled, his skin prickling as Myollnir inched closer. He seized his guitar, and a rush of energy filled him like an addictive drug. The electric haze in his vision intensified, and the world around him tinted blue. He grinned.

Tristan looked at Tor suspiciously. "Frida? Are you all right?"

Never been better. Tor concentrated. He raised his hand and attacked Myollnir's strings aggressively. His caged energy freed, his fingertips tingled and his hands glowed, pulsing with an electric shimmer.

Tristan scrambled off the couch. "What the—!"

The melody of "War Edda" blared from the amplifier. An electric surge drove through the cable, overloading the device. The amplifier exploded, but the electric current continued though the circuitry in the walls. The lights flickered, dimmed, browned, then finally fizzled out. Darkness. The muffled sounds of the confused crowd outside in the bar began to rise.

"Damn it! I can't see!" Tristan swore. "Tor! I'm going to kill you!"

Someone grabbed Tor's hand then pulled him away. "Now's our cue to leave," Luca's masculine voice said. "I know another way out."

Tor blindly followed Luca, who seemed to know exactly where he was going. He didn't stumble or bump into anything along the way. Finally, Tor heard the sounds of a metal door opening, and he was welcomed by dim moonlight and the rush of the mild night air.

"Come on!" Luca pulled Tor outside into an alley behind the Giant's Tap. They navigated out to the main street, but it seemed darker than usual, other than the cars' headlights and taillights. The sounds of honking cars echoed in the night. The streets were congested with standstill traffic.

Tor looked at an intersection and noticed the traffic light was out. The streetlights were out, too. Even the buildings and shops were dark. "What's going on?" Tor asked as they rushed down the street.

"Looks like a blackout," Luca said. "Quick thinking, Tor! It was a perfect way to get out of there."

"I didn't mean to do that."

"Sure, you didn't."

Tor rolled his eyes. There was no sense in arguing. At least he had his guitar back. And he could finally be rid of this ridiculous disguise once and for all. After tonight, he vowed to apologize again to Frida for ever thinking women had it easy.

Chapter Thirteen

Tor had been lucky enough to score tickets to Valhalla Injection only twice in his lifetime, and even though they were in the nosebleed sections, they were two of the most thrilling days of his life. But now, at long last, he was in the wings of the Blackstone Amphitheatre, about to walk out in front of an audience of twenty thousand people from all over the world.

The current band performing—Ravensworn, a trio of women from Shoreline—shook the audience with their melodic mix of blood-pumping death metal threaded with Nordic folk music. One of them used her powers to project holographic images of mythical beasts, which flew around the stage in a dazzling display, acting out the lyrics of the three songs they played. The women were good, and they were well on their way to being chosen among the top five finalists for the Battle of the Bands competition.

Tor's heart pounded. There were four bands left to perform until the finalists were announced. In addition to the previous talented bands that had already performed, VanAesir would be contending with the remaining bands. Crax, the six-member band from Montlake, had an exceptional rhythm guitarist who knew how to pump the crowd. Nifelheim's Wish, the trio from Beacon Hill, had a drummer whose inhuman speed put Luca's skills to shame. The lead singer of Purple Troll, the group from Delridge, was a multi-award winner and had done collaborations with big-time artists. Jotnar Malice had yet to perform.

Over the years, Jotnar Malice and VanAesir had proved themselves to be evenly matched in talent and skill—and their rivalry had finally led them to this day. Whoever triumphed at Valhalla Injection would also rule the underground scene.

Tor leaned his back against a steel structure behind the stage and sighed. As he slowly ran his hand up Myollnir's neck, he stared at the dots of multi-colored lights that reflected off its smooth polished surface. He needed to stay in control now, more than ever. After all the trouble they'd gone through to get Myollnir back, his friends would never forgive him if he screwed up yet again. It would suck big time if Jotnar Malice managed to make it to the finals instead of them.

A gentle touch on his bare bicep made him tense. He glanced down at the slender, chestnut-toned hand adorned in golden rings and black-painted nails. His eyes traveled up to Frida's smiling face. Tor liked that she was smiling more, whether it was his doing or because she'd finally decided to lower some of her icy walls.

"Ready for this?" she asked, her dark-brown eyes glittering with anticipation.

Tor nodded. "As ready as I'll ever be."

She paused a beat. "Whatever happens, we'll be in it together."

"Does that mean you won't quit the band if I go berserk again?"

Her eyes narrowed, and her smile broadened. "After that talk we had, I now understand that your berserk state means that you are in a state of musical bliss. It means you are wholly dedicated to your craft. You're probably the mot passionate and dedicated of all of us.

"This is who you are and who you'll always be. You're a good man with a big heart, and it'll be a cold day in Helheim before I walk away from our awesome band. Let's do this, Tor."

"Yes, let's do this." Luca squeezed between the two of them and rested his arms on their shoulders. "Because we need to win that money and get ourselves a record deal so we can finally be legit."

Giving Luca the stink eye, Frida wriggled his arm off. "It's not just about the money. It's about our career. Our future."

Luca threw his head back and laughed. "You won't say that once you're holding fifteen thousand dollars in your hand."

Ravensworn ended its last song, and the amphitheater erupted in a thunderous roar. Tor's skin prickled as beads of sweat formed on the back of his neck. *Now or never.*

Time seemed to stand still as Ravensworn exited the stage and the emcee introduced VanAesir. The stage was set. Stepping out under the hot lights, Tor gazed out into the shadows of the massive crowd.

"VanAesir! VanAesir!" the audience chanted, growing louder and louder.

Tor smiled and looked sidelong to Frida adjusting the neck strap of her bass with her usual steely calm, then behind him to Luca, who shifted on his stool behind his drum set, nervously twirling his drumsticks.

Somewhere in the crowd, the scouts and agents were watching, waiting. This was VanAesir's moment. The moment Tor had waited for all his life. *Don't fuck this up.*

Luca grasped his sticks, raised them in the air, and tapped them together, setting the tempo. Then the band broke out into the dark, rolling intro to "Odin's Vengeance."

"Blackened skies, raining blood, drowning souls in the crimson flood..." Tor was at one with Myollnir, riding its strings as he marched around the stage, letting the music envelop him. He passed near Frida, and their eyes met briefly. A small smile parted her lips.

She's counting on me, he thought, smiling back. No matter how much he'd pissed her off, she'd never turned her back on him. He marched back across the stage, returning to his world as he bobbed his head to the tempo, his long hair whipping across his face.

"The village burns, the demons' fodder. Innocents brought to the slaughter," Tor growled in a low, guttural voice into the standing microphone. His mind drifted to the voids of his subconscious, the real world around him disappearing. The faceless giant emerged from the snowy ground, looming before him. It was alone this time, much to Tor's relief and confusion of what would be in store for him this time. *Will the others be back?*

"Children of Odin, heed the call. To the wretched evil, we bring the fall..."

Tor's mind flickered from the real world to the mythic world, until they seemed to come together as one. He was suddenly in an arena—an open-air coliseum—surrounded by a massive crowd. The skies swirled with dark clouds, the ominous sight sending shivers of delight through his bones.

"Axes fly, bathed in souls. From the ashes, the bell tolls..."

Tor's vision became clear as he gazed upon the giant. The creature watched him, waiting, its eyes glowing a deep crimson. A chilly wind whisked over Tor's bare shoulder, and he shivered again. The clouds swirled faster into a dark vortex. White light flashed from within the clouds, followed by a gentle rumble of thunder.

"In the eye of the Allfather, the end is near. Take up arms in this pool of fear..."

Tor watched as the giant lumbered toward him, one hand gripping its massive battle-axe, which dripped in crimson liquid. Tor looked toward the crowd in the coliseum, the image becoming an electric haze that wavered from the mythical world to reality. For a moment, Tor found himself back at the amphitheater under the hot stage lights. The bloodthirsty onlookers wavered into head-banging fans. He glanced at his hands, which strummed Myollnir's strings autonomously. Electricity flooding his body joined with the energy surging from his fingertips into Myollnir. His skin prickled from the increased electrical charge.

"The world is drenched in the flames of time. Drive these demons back to Muspelheim..."

Tor's vision wavered again, back to his mythical world. He looked right into the eyes of the giant, who swung its mighty axe in a mad frenzy. Tor's heart pounded, goose bumps prickling his skin. His vision tinted blue, and the swirling skies responded to his charged emotion. A bolt of lightning shot down with a thunderous boom, supercharging Tor and giving him a rush like no other. He felt his mind and body yearning to let go, to unleash the full power of the storm. But in that moment, he returned to reality and caught Frida's watchful gaze out of the corner of his eye. He was made aware of his power, unlike before. He felt more in control. *She's counting on me to keep it in control.*

He closed his eyes and screamed out the chorus. *"Let their corpses rot in their everlasting flames! The Allfather watches, vengeance reins!"*

Streaks of lightning tore through the mythical world's dark skies, raining down on Tor and engulfing him in raw power. He willed the electrical field to do his bidding. His eyes locked on to the giant as the creature swung its axe. The weapon came down.

Not this time. Tor extended his hand toward the incoming blade, unleashing the full force of the storm from his fingertips. The blade impacted his hand, but something prevented it from penetrating. Lightning enveloped the giant, perfectly conducted through the metal axe head. The creature let out a harrowing roar and disintegrated to a flurry of powdery snow, which was quickly carried off in a passing wind.

The coliseum crowd cheered, and the deafening roar overtook the howling storm winds. Tor blinked again, and he was back in Washington, playing the song's outro. His hands tingled, pulsing from the electric charge within Myollnir as it glowed and crackled with energy. The audience chanted louder, demanding more. Tor looked around. Luca had his drumsticks raised, and the amps, still completely intact, throbbed with the reverb from their final chord. Had they gotten through the entire song? He glanced at Frida and Luca. Both of them grinned happily, giving him a thumbs-up.

Tor beamed at his screaming fans. He and his band had gotten through their first song without a hitch. Now, he wondered, if they continued this streak of good luck, what would be in store for them if they made it to the finals?

Chapter Fourteen

His jaw clenched, Tristan watched from backstage as the emcee announced the final-round contestants. Sweat still poured down his face from their exhausting performance, as Jotnar Malice had wowed their fans and hopefully impressed the judges with the new, exclusive songs they'd practiced specifically for the competition. Jotnar Malice was sure to be among the finalists. They were the most original. Most unique. And they had the most vocal, avid fans.

"And the scores are in! What amazing talent we have right here in our backyard! These five bands will be performing in the final round for a chance at the grand prize and to be dubbed this year's Battle of the Bands winner!" the emcee shouted into the microphone. "First up, we've got Nifelheim's Wish!"

The crowd cheered in response. Tristan's body stiffened.

"Ravensworn!" the emcee announced next, followed by another wave of cheers and screams.

Tristan clenched and unclenched his fist then finally held it steady with his other hand.

"Wolfsbane Synergy!"

Tristan swallowed a lump in his throat.

"Warchance!"

Tristan listened to his fast-beating heart, which seemed to overtake the sound of the roaring crowd. He sucked in a breath and closed his eyes. *One more spot...*

"And last but not least... VanAesir!"

Tristan deflated, his eyes shooting open wide as the audience went wild. *What!*

"Damn it!" Zeke punched the bottom of a steel light pole, creating a dented imprint of his knuckles.

"Hmph. Why am I not surprised?" Scarlet said, crossing her arms.

"Well, I am," Eric said, adjusting his earplugs. "We were the only ones who had new shit. That should've impressed the judges and scouts enough to know that we're always putting out new material. We've been robbed. Cheated!"

"Their loss," Dahlia said.

While his bandmates continued grumbling among themselves, Tristan eyed Tor and his group from across the way, celebrating and shouting in victory. Members from some of the other bands converged around them, congratulating them. Tristan narrowed his eyes. *We've worked ten times harder than them. We should be the ones celebrating right now. Those bastards should be surrounding us. Congratulating* us!

He'd already been duped, made a fool and laughingstock after Tor and Luca's ridiculous and embarrassing stunt. Tristan was not about to have his music career outdone by them, too. *If we're not good enough for those judges, then VanAesir won't be, either.* He returned to his chattering friends.

"I guess that's it for us, then." Zeke sighed.

Tristan glared. "No, I'm not giving up. We are a hundred times better than VanAesir. I'll make the judges see that they made a big mistake picking them as finalists."

"How?" Scarlet shrugged. "Not like we can stop VanAesir from performing now."

Tristan smirked. "Watch me."

Dahlia rolled her eyes. "Yeah, and we all saw how that turned out." She snickered, and Zeke, Eric, and Scarlet joined in.

Tristan's left eye twitched. Memories of yesterday's embarrassing flub haunted him like a bad dream. He'd pawned off the earrings as soon as he had the chance and burned everything he'd collected over the years—items Frida had touched, from napkins, to pens, to hair ties. He wanted her out of his mind and out of his life. Forever. Her cute game of cat-and-mouse had stopped being fun when she'd turned it into treachery, taking advantage of his vulnerable heart. She was no longer the beautiful goddess he'd adored. She was an ugly, conniving, black-hearted troll that he would be more than happy to see fall through the depths of Helheim. "We're not going to talk about that," Tristan finally said through clenched teeth. "If we can't win, then neither will VanAesir."

"Can you imagine those bastards rubbing that fifteen-grand prize and record deal in our faces if they win?" Zeke said.

Eric scowled. "Yeah, we won't hear the end of it from Luca, no doubt. What's the plan, Tristan?"

"In the finals, each band has ten minutes to perform, no matter what," Tristan explained, pointing to a large digital countdown clock at the foot of the stage. "It'd be a shame if VanAesir ends up with shitty luck and has technical difficulties during their performance." He smirked at Dahlia. "Perhaps some sound issues."

A broad smile formed on Dahlia's lips. "I can add a little static to their performance."

Tristan nodded. "Judges are looking at overall performance, originality, musical prowess, and crowd reaction. If VanAesir sounds too unbearable to hear, the judges will *have* to give low scores."

Scarlet smirked. "Or disqualify them."

Tristan nodded. "Exactly. What producer wants to take a chance on a group that's not easy on the ears and is notorious for fucking up expensive sound equipment? It's payback time." Cracking his knuckles, he acknowledged Zeke, Eric, and Scarlet. "You three keep an eye out for security."

Zeke rubbed his hands together. "This is gonna be good."

The final round proved to be competitive, as each of the top five bands upped their game, playing only their most popular songs. VanAesir was the last band to perform. Tristan observed as they got set up, noting the location for each piece of sound equipment. He followed the thick wires with his eyes to a large black trailer with a sign that read Audio/Visual. Staff Only.

The stage lights descended on the members of VanAesir. The audience let out a deafening cheer as the band prepared to dazzle the crowd a final time. They broke out into "War Edda" and had the audience bobbing and headbanging to the beat. Tristan pointed out the audio/visual trailer to his bandmates. "There's where we stop them. Dahlia, can you fiddle with the wires?"

"Of course, I can. I'll need some cover, though. Too many people walking around." She paused, looking over her bandmates a moment, then she hooked her arm with Zeke's and dragged him along. "C'mon."

"Watch for my signal, Zeke," Tristan said.

Eric pressed his fingers against his earplugs. Apparently, the plugs only suppressed a small amount of noise for his intense hearing. "Ugh, I hate this part."

Scarlet slapped Eric's shoulder, and he jolted. "You'll live."

Dahlia swept into a darkened area between the stage and the side of the trailer. Zeke stood nearby, chatting with a mixed group of people from other bands. Zeke occasionally looked in Tristan's direction.

A dim white glow flashed from the dark area between the trailer, and for a moment, Tristan spotted Dahlia kneeling with her hands placed over the wires that ran through a small opening near the trailer's door. The flash ended, and she was once again shrouded in darkness.

Suddenly, an eerie staticky sound resonated from the stage. The band members in the area halted, looking around, confused, then murmurs began to rise. The jumble of static morphed into an ear-piercing squeal. Tristan watched VanAesir from backstage. Tor was sweating bullets, and the usual high-strung energetic strut around the stage he did whenever he was enveloped in his songs was nothing more than shaky, hesitant steps. Frida and Luca exchanged worried glances then watched their bandleader, but they didn't stop playing. The voices of the roaring crowd lessened. People backstage clapped their hands over their ears. Tristan could only imagine the audience and judges were doing the same. VanAesir had two minutes left.

Still playing, Tor looked at his guitar then at the amp. The squealing sounds intensified, becoming a high-pitched screech coming from the speakers. Cringing, Tristan put a hand to his ear. He signaled to Zeke with the other for Dahlia to stop. Zeke gave a faint nod, sidling away from the group of chatting band members and making a subtle gesture toward the darkened area near the trailer.

The ear-wrenching sound fizzled out from the speakers, eventually producing echoing pops. VanAesir abruptly ended their song with nine seconds left on the clock. Confused chatter and commotion erupted throughout the crowd as Tor and his friends exchanged confused, worried glances with each other. The countdown clock reached zero, and the emcee rushed out.

"Wow, what a time to have technical difficulties! Let's see what the judges have to say!"

Chapter Fifteen

Tor stared warily at the spotlighted panel of five judges who sat at a table front and center of the stage. His heart pounded as they began entering their scores for VanAesir's shitty performance. Tor had never felt more in control of his powers, yet again, it seemed they still couldn't get through a song without problems. Myollnir sounded different. Was it his powers again? He couldn't remember. One minute, he was lost in his dream world; the next, his ears were ringing from the speakers' screeching sounds. Frida and Luca wouldn't forgive him if he screwed things up again.

The scores lit up across the board in front of the judges' seats: a total of thirteen out of a possible fifty points. A mix of cheers and boos resonated from the crowd. Tor slumped his shoulders. None of the other previous finalist bands got below forty points. VanAesir was automatically eliminated.

Tor gritted his teeth, clenching his fists. If only he could've stayed in control till the very end! He yanked the wire out of his guitar and stormed off the stage. He looked around for something to punch but found nothing. He ignored the curious looks he'd gotten from some of the other bands who were still lingering behind the stage.

Tor paced around, trying to figure out what had happened, trying to think of what to say to his friends about his apparent screwup.

"Hey." A hand touched his shoulder.

Tor froze and glanced at Frida's smiling face.

"You did good out there. We all did."

Luca came up behind her and huffed. "Just our luck we're the ones to have technical difficulties right at our grand finale!"

Tor sighed. "I'm sorry, guys. I fucked up again…"

"What?" Frida's brow wrinkled. "You didn't do anything. Something was up with the damned sound system. But I guess our band's been notorious for things like that happening; it seemed inevitable. The judges didn't seem too keen on it…"

Tor shrugged. "Can you blame them?"

"It wasn't our fault this time." Luca shook his fist. "We should get a do-over."

Frida shook her head. "Don't worry about it, Luca. There's always next year."

If *we get tickets, or if Harold manages to pull some strings again.* Tor tried to smile at her optimism. But he couldn't get over the feeling that he'd let his friends down. They'd practiced so hard, and he couldn't even keep things in control.

Luca sighed. "I guess you're right. I mean, this was our first time we got to play at Valhalla Injection, and we ended up making it all the way to the finals in the Battle of the Bands!"

"If we were good enough to make it this far this year, then next year, we'll go even further." Frida grinned.

Tor's gaze bounced from Luca to Frida. "You think so?"

Frida nodded. "And I was impressed that you managed to keep it all together. I'm proud of you, Tor."

Tor attempted a small smile. It wasn't often he heard a genuine compliment from Frida, and he cherished it like a precious diamond.

"And as for quitting the band," Frida continued. "As I said before, it'd be a cold day in Helheim before I ever do that. We've gone through so much together over the years. And, yeah, sometimes you guys piss me off, but you're still my friends—my family. Nothing will ever change that."

An invigorating feeling filled Tor's chest, and he smiled proudly. "Thanks, Fri."

"I love you, too, Fri!" Luca hugged her from behind.

Frida elbowed Luca in the chest, and Luca released her, grinning sheepishly.

"And the winner is… Wolfsbane Synergy!" the emcee announced. The entire amphitheater erupted in a deafening cheer.

The tribal-tattooed quintet walked out on stage, their silver chains, buttons, and numerous buckles on their belts and leather vests reflecting the lights.

Tor sighed, giving a half-hearted clap. He'd known them when they were just an up-and-coming garage band two years ago. Now they were on their way to a record deal. Hanging his head, he turned and trudged toward the parking lot.

"Hey."

Tor halted again, his ears burning at the sound of Tristan's voice. Scowling at a pair of familiar-looking brown motorcycle boots, Tor raised his head and stared into the eyes of his nemesis. "What do *you* want?"

Tristan nodded to him. "Just wanted to congratulate you on making it as far as you did."

Tor blinked several times. *Am I dreaming, or did I actually hear a compliment from Tristan Westgard?* "Say what?"

Tristan rolled his eyes and half-smiled. "Hey, I know we've had our differences and all, but Valhalla Injection is a big deal, and you guys were amazing to make it all the way to the finals."

Frida crossed her arms and narrowed her eyes. "What are you up to, Tristan?"

Luca mimicked her. "Yeah, what are you up to, Tristan?"

Tristan shrugged. "Is it so strange for me to show a little sportsmanship now and again for my rival?"

Tor lifted an eyebrow. "From you? Yes." He noticed out of the corner of his eye that the rest of Jotnar Malice were slowly closing in on him, Frida, and Luca. His body shuddered, and a strange electric sensation filled his body, making the hair on his arms react. Streaks of lightning ran down his arms then disappeared.

"Well, then how about a truce?" Tristan stuck out his hand. "We have fans who love us both. Maybe we can think about doing that collab album one of these days, eh?"

Tor stared at the extended hand with uncertainty. Tristan was right about one thing. They shared some of the same fans. It could perhaps be an interesting experience working together to further build that fanbase. Both bands would benefit in the end. Tor couldn't believe the impossible just may happen. "Maybe," Tor finally said, quirking a small smile. He extended his hand, as well.

Tristan's face darkened, and he suddenly cocked his hand back in a tight fist. "Or maybe not." He launched his fist toward Tor's face.

Shit! Tor's skin prickled, as though he could feel the energy of the incoming blow. In a flash, Tor lifted his hand and caught Tristan's fist when it was inches from his left eye.

Tristan started, shock reeling his bug-eyed face. Tor felt the tingle of static charge leaving his hand. The metal chains and accessories Tristan wore were perfect conductors. Tristan grunted and tremored as the electric current surged through him, then he was tossed back several feet. His bandmates rushed to their fallen leader.

"Tristan! Are you all right?" Scarlet called, kneeling over him.

Tristan mumbled something incoherent, his body still twitching.

Tor watched them with narrowed eyes. As he closed his fist, small streaks of electricity threaded over his knuckles. "Anyone else?"

Zeke stood and took a step forward, but Scarlet grabbed his pant leg, stopping him.

"Are you crazy?" she muttered to her comrade through clenched teeth.

Scowling, Zeke stood down.

"Let's get out of here," Eric said.

The band helped Tristan up and carried him off. Scarlet glared over her shoulder at Tor and his friends. "This isn't over."

Tor watched his rivals retreat with their leader. *For now, it is.*

"Those assholes!" Frida growled. She looked at Tor. "Are you all right?"

"He's fine." Smirking, Luca slapped Tor's shoulder. "That was awesome, by the way, man. You've got some lightning reflexes. My influence must be rubbing off on you."

"Let's go find Harold before anything else happens," Frida said.

Tor sighed. "I don't want to deal with more of Harold's berating."

Luca pointed to someone rushing toward them. "Looks like you don't have a choice."

Harold was huffing and out of breath, a layer of sweat beading over his brow. "We need to talk."

Tor shoved his hands in his pockets and averted his gaze. *He's probably gonna resign from managing us...*

"It wasn't Tor's fault this time, Harold!" Frida said. "The stupid sound system—"

"We totally sucked in the finals," Luca added. "Our one chance at going places is ruined forever. I guess our career is done for good, huh?"

Harold folded his arms, a hint of a smile on his lips. "Oh, I wouldn't say that."

Tor's ears perked, and he looked at his manager with a raised eyebrow. "What are you talking about, man?"

"Opportunities come and go. A musician's career isn't always guaranteed. It's all about how bad you want it."

"Hey, we practiced our asses off," Luca said. "Did you not hear us in Valhalla Injection?"

Harold nodded. "Of course I did. You guys were phenomenal. So much, in fact, I just got through meeting with an agent who wants to chat with you three."

THE END

About the Author

Marie Long is a novelist who enjoys the snowy weather, the mountains, and a cup of hot white chocolate. She's an avid supporter of literacy movements. To learn more about her, visit her website: www.marielongauthor.com.